P9-DTB-251

HIPPOMOBILE!

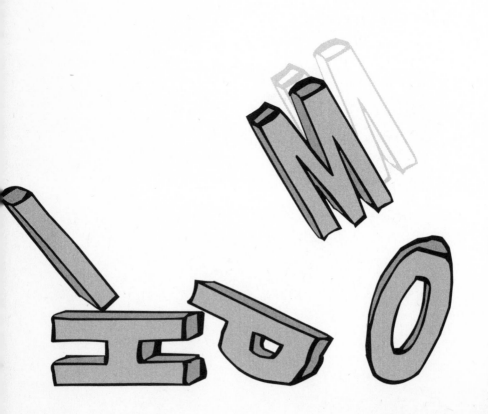

OBILE!

By JEFF TAPIA

CLARION BOOKS ❁ Houghton Mifflin Harcourt

Boston   New York

CLARION BOOKS

215 Park Avenue South

New York, New York 10003

Clarion Books is an imprint of
Houghton Mifflin Harcourt Publishing Company.

www.hmhbooks.com

The text was set in ITC Stone.

Map art by Andrew Glass

Design by Sharismar Rodriguez

Library of Congress Cataloging-in-Publication Data

Tapia, Jeff.

Hippomobile! / by Jeff Tapia.

pages cm

Summary: Ten-year-old twins Jimmy and Stella start a campaign
to save their dying small town by restoring the amazing hippomobile,
an old-fashioned vehicle made out of a horse wagon.

ISBN 978-0-547-99548-9 (hardcover)

[1. City and town life—Fiction. 2. Vehicles—History—Fiction.
3. Brothers and sisters—Fiction. 4. Twins—Fiction. 5. Old age—Fiction.
6. Humorous stories.] I. Title.

PZ7.T16365Hi 2013

[Fic]—dc23   2012041303

Manufactured in the United States of America

DOC 10 9 8 7 6 5 4 3 2 1

4500435284

For Agnes and Eva

CONTENTS

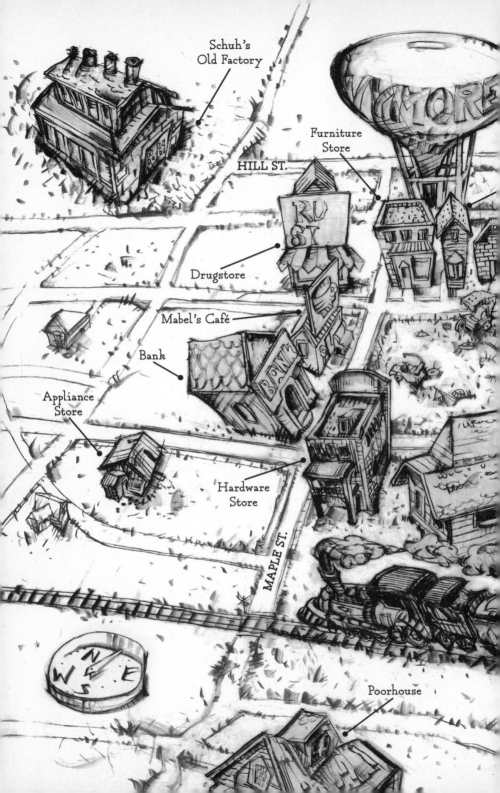

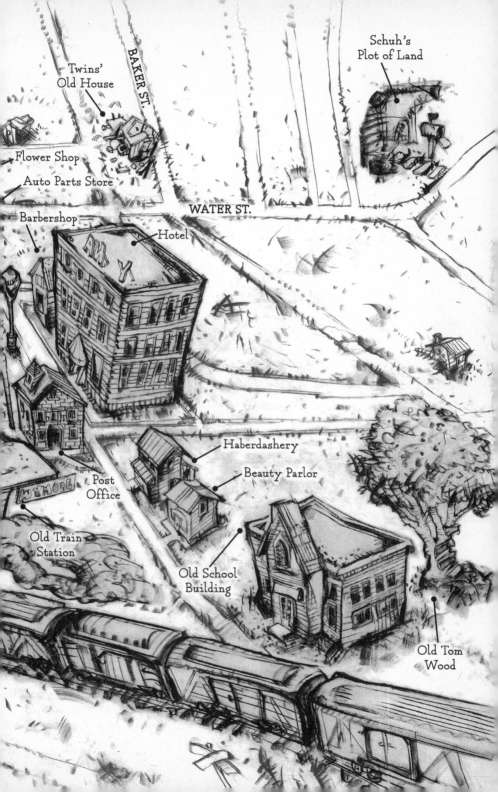

HIPPOMOBILE!

Chapter One:

Welcome to Nowhere

YOU AIN'T GONNA BELIEVE this, but it's true. We're the last two kids in town. In fact, we're the *only* two kids in town. And what's more, since we're twins, it's almost like there ain't even two of us, even though there is. One of us is Jimmy and the other one is Stella, and we don't look too much alike, like some twins do.[1]

We live in the town of Wymore, and Wymore is so small you might as well not even try to find it on a map. The official population is only fifty-one, and that number drops down to forty-nine in the summertime when Pops is on the road and Mom is working what she calls the graveyard shift far off in another county, and we're left here to live with our remaining forty-seven grandmas and grandpas.[2]

Now, a long time back, Wymore had lots more people in it and a real train station where ladies in funny hats and gentlemen with long curly mustaches got off. There was

. . . .

1 Even though we got the same bowl cuts.
2 We'll explain that one later.

also real stores where you could buy stuff, and even a shoe factory we're gonna tell you about real soon. For now, we'll just tell you that people used to travel right far to buy Gottfried Schuh's Everlasting Shoes. And on account of how far they had to go to get here, some of them folks would stay overnight at the one hotel in town. Back then it was glamorous and shiny as spit and called the Stanley Hotel, until over time the *S*, the *T*, the *L*, and the *E* on the sign rusted and fell off. Then it became the Any Hotel.[3] That's where everybody in Wymore lives now, and seeing that there ain't but twenty-five rooms, we've all got to squeeze together some and double up and just plain make do.

Last summer we lived in Room #9 because we were nine years old back then. Meanwhile we've moved across the hall to Room #10, and you can probably guess how come. The mattresses are worse there, and the pillows are harder, and the floor squeaks more, and there's no picture in the picture frame up between our two beds, but the screen in the window don't let in no bugs, and now we can overlook the whole town square. Not that much ever happens down there, but if it does, we ain't gonna miss it.

The hotel has three floors, and we're on the middle

. . . .

3 Which today has another new name you'll learn about soon enough.

floor. And when it's not too hot and muggy at night, we sometimes climb up on the roof and pitch a tent. The roof's so flat that there ain't no chance of us rolling off it in our sleep. But for the longest time, Mom used to get the all-overs[4] about it because of how she was so scared of heights.[5] And so we just didn't bother to tell her when we went up there.

Except for the hotel, there ain't really anyplace left to go to in Wymore outside of Mabel's Café. All the other places that used to be in Wymore are all closed down now. Like there used to be an appliance store and a flower shop and a bank, but they're gone. And there used to be an auto parts store and a hardware store and a beauty salon, but they're gone. And there used to be a furniture store and a drugstore and a haberdashery,[6] but they're gone. And there used to be a barbershop, but that's gone too, although Grandpa Homer and Grandpa Virgil still have their barbershop duet.

Sometimes we go and play in them old stores, though, especially in summer when days go by slower than a snail

. . . .

4   That means she got nervous.
5   That's one of the things that was gonna change over the course of this summer.
6   That's what they used to call a men's clothing store.

riding a turtle. The old furniture store is good for playing tag in on account of all the old busted tables and chairs you can jump over, and there's a rusty stove at the appliance store that we can bake a dust-and-pebble pie in if we feel like. Sometimes we go to the old drugstore and cough and sneeze and take our temperature with a twig under our armpit and swallow medicine we make ourselves by rolling up little balls of yellow newspaper.[7]

Robbing the old bank is another way to pass the time around here, but our play money is running low and there ain't many grandmas and grandpas left who can stick 'em up, on account of how their arms just don't move easy anymore. Sometimes we go to the haberdashery and dress up in old, too big, ugly clothes if Grandpa Bert lets us. And sometimes we just think about how nice it'd be to go swimming, but Wymore ain't got a swimming pool. There ain't even a swimming hole somewhere. The town is all dirt and dust and wind and no water.

That leaves Mabel's. The café is named after Grandma Mabel, and there ain't no one around who can swing a wood spoon like her. And alls you gotta do is taste her

. . . .

7 We've found out there's only so much old newspaper medicine you can swallow before you get a stomachache.

checkerboards[8] or her Bossy in a bowl[9] or a slice of her Eve with a lid on,[10] and you'll be a customer for life, if not longer.

Now, you might've noticed we ain't said nothing about there being a school in Wymore. Well, you would've noticed right, because there ain't one. There is an old school building one block off the town square, right next to the old oak tree everybody around here refers to as Old Tom Wood, but there just ain't enough kids around here to fill up a school, and so it long since closed its doors. Think about it. How would you like having just two kids in your class and one of them being your sister and the other one being your brother?

But that doesn't mean we get to not go to school. We go five long days a week, nine long months a year, just like you do. In fact, this summer we even got homework. And pretty soon Mr. Buzzard will be coming through town every morning bright and early in his yellow pickup[11] to collect us in front of Mabel's. We sit out back in a wore-out

. . . .

8 That's what we call waffles.
9 And that's beef stew.
10 That's apple pie with a top crust. We ain't sure exactly how all these foods got named, but it's just one thing you're gonna have to get used to.
11 It used to be red, but we got to help him paint it yellow because everybody knows that's the color of a school bus.

tire with our bait cans[12] in our laps, and he drives us over nine miles of back roads that give our bones a good rattling. School's up in a place called McFall. That's the big city around here, with the one traffic light and a general store.

But we still got some time left to laze about up in Old Tom Wood and ruminate over all that happened this summer. We know our teacher is gonna be asking us what we did, and we wanna be good and ready when she does. Because a summer like ours don't happen but once in a blue moon, especially them six days that changed the course of our lives and the lives of everyone else here in Wymore on account of something called a hippomobile. And here's the story the two of us wanna tell.

· ·

12 That's what we call lunch boxes. Which is pretty weird on account of that nobody in Wymore has ever gone fishing since there ain't no water to fish in.

Chapter Two:

Leatherbread and Goozlum

IT ALL STARTED AT Mabel's one morning earlier this summer. We can't remember if it was a Monday or a Tuesday or a Friday, but it don't make much difference anyhow because the days are all the same around here.

We do know for sure it was morning, though, because we were sitting right across from each other in our favorite window booth[1] over steaming plates of leatherbread and goozlum and crispy overland trout. And if you're wondering what kinda food that is, alls it is, is pancakes, maple syrup, and bacon. But it tastes way better when you call it leatherbread and goozlum and overland trout, and if you ask us, you should take to calling it that yourselves.

Anyway, we were busy filling our shirts, and Grandma Ida, the waitress at Mabel's, came up to us and said, "You two sure do know how to play a mean knife and fork."

. . . .

1 It's our favorite because the seats don't sag too much in the middle and we don't have to see the TV set that's mounted up in the corner and always tuned in to the weather report.

Which was her way of saying how hungry we ate. Then she asked us if we'd like another black cow.[2]

"Yes, please, Grandma Ida," we said.

"Well, then, make use of them bibs[3] of yours, and I'll go milk Bessie."

So we wiped off our brown mustaches and then cleaned our plates until they shined so much they made you squint.

Grandma Ida came back with a tray balanced high up over her head. She was one heckuva soup jockey[4] all right, and everybody in Wymore appreciated her, us and Mom and Pops probably most of all. Because without Grandma Ida promising to keep a fine eye on us, Mom never could've taken that summer job she needed in order for us to make ends meet.[5]

Last summer was the first summer she went away. The morning Mr. Buzzard came to drive her off, her faucets

• •

2 You can probably figure that one out for yourself.
3 Bibs is just napkins around here, not them things babies wear around their necks.
4 A waitress. Mom don't think it sounds very nice, but Grandma Ida says she don't mind it.
5 We used to think it was "ends meat" and was something like meat loaf that you gotta eat when your money runs out. Now we know better.

leaked something awful,[6] and we almost had to roll up the bottoms of our pants. But we all got used to it over time, and Mom eventually stopped calling every hour to see how we was doing and whether we'd skinned a knee or got bit by a bug. So the day she left this summer wasn't half as big a deal, but of course we're ten now.

Anyhow, Grandma Ida came back and served us our tall drinks and said, "We're sure lucky with that ol' gal. Ain't many cows left will give you chocolate milk these days."

Grandma Ida always made that same joke, and we always smiled and said, "Thank you, Grandma Ida." Because Pops says there ain't nothing like a good pair of manners.

"So what kinda trouble you two planning on getting into today?" Grandma Ida asked, and gave us a wink.

And, in fact, we'd just been discussing that very same topic. We were figuring on climbing Old Tom Wood and then maybe seeing if Grandma Winnie would take us for a spin in her golf cart. All our grandmas and grandpas used golf carts to get around town, since there wasn't no one left in Wymore to fix their cars once they broke down. And

· ·

6 That means she cried a lot, and maybe our faucets leaked a drop or
two as well.

that's how come there was so many clunkers rusting away on the square, their tires flat, their windows busted, and their fenders dropped clean off.

"We ain't sure, Grandma Ida. You got any ideas for us?" we asked.

"Well, lemme think," she said. And she rested her dishrag over her shoulder and looked up at the cracks in the ceiling and them two brown splotches that looked like a tricycle and a boat.[7] Then she snapped her fingers and said, "I got it! Why don't you do your homework?"

And we said, "Aww, Grandma Ida!" And now you know we weren't kidding about her keeping a fine eye on us.

"I ain't the one who assigned it to you," she said. "And, besides, we've all had to go through it."

That was true enough. It was school tradition going all the way back to when our grandmas and grandpas were our age that kids starting the fifth grade had to memorize all the presidents over the summer. And not just the names, but they had to be in the right order, too. It was the perfect way to ruin your vacation worse than a dropped egg.

. . . .

7   We used to think someone had spilled coffee up on the ceiling. But Grandma Ida told us they were just water stains from a leak in the roof.

"Can't we do something else?" we asked. "We already learned the first two by heart."

"Who are they, then?" Grandma Ida set a hand on her hip like she could tell we were putting on the bluff.

"George Washington and Tom Adams," we said.

Grandma Ida looked at the ceiling again and sighed something awful. "*John* Adams."

"Stella, I told you it wasn't Tom!"

"Maybe you did, Jimmy James. But you didn't say it was John, neither."

We were on the verge of getting into it, but Grandma Ida pulled the fuse clean out of us when she said, "You know what, summer ain't that far along just yet. Why don't you go on over to the library instead and get yourselves a book and climb up Old Tom Wood and read for a while."

At last we found something we could all agree on.

Chapter Three:

Things Worth Knowing

NOW, WE AIN'T SAID nothing about Wymore having a library. And it's true, there ain't one, at least not a real one. Alls there is, is a pile of books all jumbled up in some milk crates a few booths down, right there at Mabel's. So when Grandma Ida suggested us to go to the library, alls we had to do was hop on down and slide into what we call the library booth.

A long time ago, things were different. We've been told Wymore used to have an honest-to-goodness library with one whole room full of books and a magazine rack full of magazines telling you how to keep your house clean and other rotten news. You even got your own library card, and there was a real live librarian, our Grandma Henrietta, who kept telling you to hold your potato. That was her way of saying to hush it no matter how hushed you already was.

But what happened was the library started falling apart, just like lots of places here in Wymore. The front door came off its hinges, and then the windows stopped opening because the building went crooked, and after that red bricks began popping out of the walls like buttons off a shirt. Then the ceiling began sagging like an old mattress, and whoever was in the library at the time grabbed their canes and ran out as fast as their bones could carry them.

Most of the books got lost in the rubble when the library caved in for good. But the few that remained got hauled off in milk crates and taken over to Mabel's. And them were the ones we were picking through now.

The problem was, by that time we'd darn near read the whole lot of them. Plus there were some books we didn't want to read at all. Because take our word for it, you could find some peculiar-sounding books in them milk crates. Like one is called *Lectures on the True, the Beautiful, and the Good,* and that has to be just about the very last thing any kid is ever gonna wanna read about. But lucky for us there's some good ones in them crates too. One of our favorites is *The Rover Twins and the Gigantic Waterfall,* and that's because it's so dang hot and dry in Wymore that not even the water fountain outside Mabel's works no more.[1] We'll read our favorite books over and over, either sitting up in Old Tom Wood's comfy branches or laying on our beds back at the hotel when the day's too dusty and you can't hardly see nothing at all outdoors, let alone read.

. . . .

1   When you press it down, it just wheezes and shoots out dust.

So we were excited as a cat-and-mouse show when our hands grabbed hold of a book we swore we ain't ever seen before. It was called *The Handy Cyclopedia of Things Worth Knowing* and was about as thick as one of Grandma Mabel's triple-decker mousetraps[2] and chock-full of all kinds of stuff you never knew you could ever know. So we couldn't get out the door quick enough.

Grandma Ida saw us and yelled, "Be back in time for lunch!"

She didn't have to tell us that. Because we knew she was serving zeppelins in a cloud, which in Wymore is sausages and mashed potatoes, and we wouldn't miss them for nothing in the world.

. . . .

2　Grilled cheese sandwiches.

Chapter Four:

How Mr. Wolfeschle-gelsteinhausen Became Grandpa Bert

BY NOW YOU'RE PROBABLY wondering how come we keep calling everybody Grandpa This and Grandma That and how anybody could ever have forty-seven grandparents. So we better be up-front with you now before we get to the exciting part where we tell you what we found in *The Handy Cyclopedia of Things Worth Knowing*.

They ain't really our real grandparents.[1] We just call them Grandpa This and Grandma That because they're all old and have either gray hair or no hair at all. And since we're the only two kids in Wymore, and Mom and Pops ain't even in Wymore during the summer, every person we come across is either gonna be a grandma or a grandpa.

But here's how we began calling them as such. It all started quite some time ago with Grandpa Bert and his last name, Wolfeschlegelsteinhausen, which ached our tongues every time we tried to say it. One hot and dusty

· ·

1 We had real grandparents living here once, but the heat finally got to them and they moved someplace colder.

day, we were outside of what used to be the post office[2] playing mailman, where one of us was the mailman and the other one of us was the barking dog. That was when Grandpa Bert cruised up in his golf cart quiet as a one-handed clap.

Grandpa Bert is the one who used to own the haberdashery. His clothes were a bit old-fashioned, and we liked the deep pockets they had because they often contained a treat or two for us. Grandpa Bert got off his golf cart and pulled out a couple of jawbreakers. We said, or at least tried to say, "Thanks, Mr. Wolfeschlegelsteinhausen." At that time he wasn't Grandpa Bert yet, although we're getting to that part right now.

His name must've come out in all the wrong order because he smiled and said, "You know what?"

And we said, "What, Mr. um . . . ?"

And he said, "Why don't you just call me Grandpa from now on. It'll be easier on all of us."

We liked that idea a lot, and we waved and called out, "Bye, Grandpa!" and jammed our jawbreakers in between our cheeks and gums as he slowly vanished in a cloud of

2 The flagpole's still there, but the flag ain't.

dust. And that was that. At least we thought that was that.

What happened next was that the other old folks in town heard about how Bert Wolfeschlegelsteinhausen was now going by Grandpa, and for some reason that really rode their britches.[3] It seems that they all wanted a piece of the grandma-and-grandpa pie. And soon, one by one, when they thought no one else was looking, they started coming up to us and pinching our cheeks and bending down toward us as best they could and saying, "Why don'tcha just call me Grandma from now on?" Or, "Wouldn't it be funner to just call me Grandpa instead of Mr. Snuggerud?"[4] And so on and so on.

That seemed fine with us. Until the next problem happened. Whenever we walked into Mabel's and said something like "Howdy, Grandpa!" or "Mornin', Grandma!" all the heads in the café would turn around.

So finally one afternoon as a majority of the town was gathered at Mabel's, enjoying one of her famous barked pies,[5] we counted to three and slid out of our booth and

. . . .

3 Which means they didn't like it none.
4 Who later became Grandpa Milton.
5 A barked pie is what we call a pie that has a crust on top. When it's done baking, it comes out looking like a piece of bark but tastes a whole lot better.

snucked over to the lunch counter and climbed up on them stools and turned off the weather report[6] and said, "Grandmas, Grandpas, we all know the forecast ain't gonna change much. It's around here that things have gotta change. So listen up, because here's what we're proposing."

And they did listen, too. The ones with hearing aids turned up the volume, and those with natural hearing cupped their hands around the back of their ears.

Our plan, as you may have figured out by now, was to start calling them Grandpa or Grandma plus their first name. Because we reckoned that if we started calling them Grandpa or Grandma plus their last name, then we'd be back to square one and the whole problem with saying "Grandpa Wolfeschlegelsteinhausen." So we asked, "Is it a deal?"

We weren't sure how they were gonna react. It's sometimes hard to change people's ways once they turn old, wrinkly, and forty. And so after we stopped talking, our eyes darted around the café to the other eyes in the café, which were also darting around the café. Nobody said a word, and for a moment it sounded as quiet as Grandma

· ·

6   The weatherman was just then pointing with his long stick at a big, fat, yellow, hot-looking sun.

Henrietta's dream library. But then all of a sudden, they all busted out laughing, and one by one they got out of their booths and lined up and told us what their first names were, and we wrote them down on the back of our paper place mats. And it's been that way ever since.[7]

---

7   We also offered to call them Aunt or Uncle Whatever, but no one took us up on it.

Chapter Five:

Rare
and
Exquisite

NOW, WHERE WERE WE? Oh, yeah, Grandma Ida was just calling after us to be back in time for lunch. We shoved our way out the screen door[1] with *The Handy Cyclopedia of Things Worth Knowing.* We were so excited about reaching Old Tom Wood, and our legs were spinning so fast, that we got to the corner of the square in record time, even in spite of the strong wind. Because the day we're talking about was blowy and gusty and gritty and dusty, like lots of our summer days are. If you ever feel like you wanna turn your teeth brown, all you gotta do around here is smile into the wind.

Pops had nailed some slats to the tree to make it easier for us to climb up. He always likes the chance of doing something with his hands aside from just gripping a steering wheel all day long. What Pops does is he drives a big rig. He says it's a big rig for big pig because he moves pork. There's even a cartoon picture of a big smiling pig on the side of his truck. It's wearing a red-and-white checkered

. . . .

1　It was always stuck and hard to open.

bib and sitting up at a dinner table, holding a fork and a knife. We always found that picture a bit unusual.

Now at the bottom of Old Tom Wood, we argued some about who was gonna climb up first. At our age being first is a big deal, and it ain't for nothing that kids often push and shove and butt in line. Except that day we were arguing about who *didn't* wanna go first because one of us had on a skirt and didn't want her brother looking up and seeing her underwear.

"Who'd wanna look up and see your gross underwear, anyway?"

"My underwear ain't gross, Jimmy James. At least it ain't half as gross as your socks are."

"My socks ain't gross."

"I'm gonna tell Mom you ain't been changing them every day like you're supposed to."

"My socks ain't gross."

"Is that all you can say?"

"Maybe they are gross, but they ain't half as gross as the way you pick your ear with your finger and then pull it back out and observe it like you was observing a rare bug."

"At least I pick mine. Have you seen the inside of your ears lately?"

We'll spare you other gross details and just say we got

over our differences and eventually made it up Old Tom Wood and sat down on our favorite big knotty branch that we always sat on.

First we got situated and pulled off a couple leafs that were full of brown holes and flicked away some ants that were already crawling on us. Then we stuck our heads together and looked at *The Handy Cyclopedia of Things Worth Knowing* that we were holding there on our laps. The cover wasn't nothing special. It just had the title on it in swirly letters and the name of the guy who wrote it, who must've been real smart to know all that stuff. And there was a date wrote at the bottom, but it was part rubbed off and just said 18-something.

Now, that's old, all right, but age ain't what made the book so special. What made it so special is when you opened it up and saw how the book had so many pages in it and how on each one of them pages there really was something worth knowing, just like the title promised.

For example, you could find in that book a list of the tallest structures in the world and tips on how to shave and twenty common French phrases and ways to yank out a loose tooth.[2] You could learn about live sponges and how

. . . .

2 On page 87, a page we would be looking back at many times very soon.

if they get chopped up, they can stick themselves back to-gether again just like new. Or you could learn curious facts about hair, like how on the average head there are about one thousand hairs to the square inch,[3] and how four hairs can hold up a one-pound weight, and how a whole head of hair could hold up an entire audience of two hundred people! Now, be honest, did you ever think you could ever know something like that? And then right after the hairy section, there was a poem by William Shakespeare you could read if you felt like it.[4]

And we ain't even said nothing about the chapter called "Weird Analogies in Nature." That's where you could discover that the English walnut is almost the exact representation of the human brain, and that black cherries resemble human eyes, and that pumpkins sometimes grow mammoth and end up looking like a person. And right after that chapter came ten whole pages of riddles![5]

We kept flipping back and forth and eventually flipped to a part in the book called "500 Useful Phrases for Eloquent

. . . .

3 Except for the bald ones in Wymore.
4 We didn't.
5 The fun thing about them was that the answers were printed upside down at the bottom of the page. And so while part of the fun was trying to guess at the answers, the other part of the fun was trying to sneak a peek at the answers without the other person catching you.

Diction." Now, when a book tells you that diction is how you talk, and eloquent is when your talk sounds good and proper, then chances are that ain't gonna be something you're gonna wanna read all too close, especially in the middle of summer. But for some reason, we didn't turn the page, and instead we ran our fingers down the long list of words and tried to enunciate the useful phrases we found there.

But whole bunches of them phrases didn't even sound English to us at all, and we finally agreed that them words just didn't exist no more.[6] We were on the verge of turning to the chapter called "The Mysteries of Hypnotism,"[7] when we spotted a few phrases that did seem kinda useful and eloquent, even to us. Maybe we secretly thought we could impress Mom, or maybe it was just that the heat was affecting our brains. But for whatever reason, we made a promise that we'd try and make use of them in our speech as much as possible, at least for the next hour or so. And here's the ones we chose:

. . . .

6   We're talking about phrases like "diurnal rotation" and "distraught air" and "minatory shadow" and "waggishly sapient."

7   We thought if we could hypnotize some of our grandparents, we could get them to tell us where they stashed their candy.

Dogged determination. That means that you never give up when you want something.

Dramatic and sensational. That's when something is a real big deal.

Rare and exquisite. You can say that for something that ain't common and ordinary and ugly.

Robust and rugged is when something is tough and don't get wore out.

But pretty soon we didn't find useful and eloquent diction all that dramatic and sensational, and our dogged determination to expand our list of phrases wasn't especially robust and rugged, especially when there were the rare and exquisite mysteries of hypnotism to be discovered.

And so pay attention right close because here's what happened next. We turned to page 237, expecting to learn how to rotate our eyes and wiggle our fingers just right so we could put our grandmas and grandpas into a trance, but instead what happened was that an old envelope that looked rare and exquisite fell out of the book and smack into our laps.

We couldn't tell at first if it was anything dramatic and sensational, thinking it might just contain an old grocery list for milk, bread, eggs, and some airtights.[8] But we had dogged determination to find out.

The envelope had a message stamped across it that said RETURN TO SENDER. ADDRESS UNKNOWN. We pulled the letter out and saw how it was old and yellow and brittle and not robust and rugged at all. We unfolded it and flattened it out as best we could, but alls we saw was a tangle of small squiggles that we figured must've been words of some sort, but not any words we could make any sense out of. The only thing we knew was that it had to be some rare and exquisite letter of some kind, and that the whole thing was right dramatic and sensational, indeed.

We must've stared at the piece of paper for longer than a summer sunset. And even then, with all the dogged determination we could muster up, we weren't able to decipher one word in it. Until suddenly we could. Right there smack-dab in the middle of that paper. And we knew right off what it meant, and we also knew right off that it really was dramatic and sensational.

The one word we finally deciphered was

Hippomobile

. . . .

8 Canned goods are called that because no air can't get in them.

Chapter Six:

Once Upon a Time

NOW, SINCE THIS STORY OF ours is mainly gonna be about the hippomobile, this is probably the best time to tell you what it is and what it ain't.

We weren't but pint-size little kids who couldn't even snap up our shirts right the day we learned about the hippomobile. It was a day we reckon we won't be forgetting anytime soon.

Grandpa Homer and Grandpa Virgil told us all about it. These grandpas are the town elders—they're well over ninety—and they're the biggest linguisters[1] Wymore has ever known. Our other grandmas and grandpas will sometimes turn down their hearing aids or even pull them straight out of their ears when they see those two coming because they know they're in for a gale of wind.[2] Sometimes what Grandpa Homer and Grandpa Virgil say is the truth you can chisel in stone. Other times they beat the truth like a blacksmith pounding hot metal.

. . . .

1 Somebody who talks a lot.
2 That's Wymore talk for a long story.

You ain't never gonna see the one without the other. The reason for that isn't because they're twins like us, but because Grandpa Homer doesn't see no more and so Grandpa Virgil's got to guide him all around town. He makes sure Grandpa Homer doesn't bump into none of the old jalopies rusting away on the square, and he also makes sure no one runs him down in their golf cart.

Grandpa Homer and Grandpa Virgil used to be the town barbers back before we were born. They cut all the men's hair in town until all them heads went bald and put Grandpa Homer and Grandpa Virgil clean out of business, except for the occasional kid haircut. They still liked to spend time in their barbershop, however, and that's where we were the day we learned about the hippomobile. Since we were young and in kindergarten at the time, we were doing little-kid stuff like wearing barber capes around our necks and flying around on push brooms like superheroes.

Grandpa Homer and Grandpa Virgil were loosening up their vocal cords because on top of talking all the time, they sang in their very own barbershop duet.[3] They even had funny-looking hats to sing in that were made out of

....

3 They couldn't find two other grandpas who could sing to make a quartet.

straw and flat on top and had a wide red ribbon going all around them and a wide brim to match.

At some point that day, Grandpa Homer and Grandpa Virgil mentioned something about the hippomobile, and we laughed ourselves silly at the sound of the word. They asked us if our Mom and Pops hadn't never told us nothing about it before. And when we said no, they shook their heads like their best milk cow had just kicked the bucket and told us to climb up in them barber chairs right quick because it was time we learned a thing or two about our heritage. We did as we were told, and we didn't have to wait long for the learning.

Grandpa Homer started doing the telling. "It all began more'n one hundred years back," he said. "In the poorhouse that used to be located, I believe, four blocks down Maple Street. Ain't that right, Virgil?"

"I believe it is, Homer. I do, indeed."

"Thank you, Virgil," Grandpa Homer said. "And back in them days, four blocks down Maple was considered way out in the boonies."

Boonies or no boonies, we hadn't ever heard of a poorhouse before, and so we asked what one was. We found out that a poorhouse is just like it sounds like it's gonna be. It's a house full of poor people who didn't have no house to live in and no job to do and no money, neither. And while they lived there, they had to do things like plant food on a little farm they had or chop wood or do just about anything they could find to do for anyone else in town so as to make a little spare change.

"It warn't no bed of roses" was how Grandpa Homer summed it up.

And Grandpa Virgil said, "You can sure as heck say that again, Homer."

Later on Grandpa Homer *would* say it again, too. But for now he continued with where he was in his story. "And it was in the Maple Street poorhouse that a young man by the name of Gottfried Schuh once lived. He was fresh off the boat from a place called Germany—"

"Hey," we said. "There ain't no boats around here."

We might've still been young at the time, but that didn't mean we were green behind the ears. We knew a boat when we saw one, and we knew we ain't ever saw one in Wymore and most likely never would. Unless it was a boat that could float on dust.

"Them kids have got you there, Homer," said Grandpa Virgil.

Grandpa Homer said, "Well, Gottfried must've got off the boat somewheres, because there warn't no airplanes back then, and he couldn't have walked here from Germany. So let's just say that at some point he got off a boat and sooner or later ended up in the town of Wymore without a penny in his pants. How's that sound?"

We thought it sounded much better, and Grandpa Virgil said, "I does like the sound of that, Homer. I really does."

"Well, then," Grandpa Homer said. "And since Gottfried Schuh didn't have any money and wasn't yet proficient in our American language, he landed in the poorhouse and labored taking care of other folks' animals and cut wood and fixed whatever anyone happened to need fixing. He did a fine job of everything he put his hands to, and eventually he caught the attention of a party of Wymore fellows set to travel to Alaska to dig for gold."

"Gold?" we shouted.

"That's right," said Grandpa Homer. "The shiny yellow stuff womenfolk hang off their ears. Whole lotta fellows back then was goin' out Alaska way lookin' for it. Wasn't they, Virgil?"

"They was, Homer. Heck, cousin of mine tried it, but the only thing he came back with was a runny nose."

Grandpa Homer said, "A place called Dawson City is where they hoped to make their good fortunes. And this Gottfried Schuh was one of 'em. On account of that he was known to be able to fix anything, right on down to a rainy day. And he was as strong as an ox, which you needed to be to carry your supplies up the snowy trails that led to the gold fields. Once you got there, you lived in a tent and ate fish for breakfast, lunch, and dinner. And that's if you were lucky. And you also froze your behind off, grew a long, dirty beard, and drank something called ice-worm cocktails."

Ice worms? We figured he was trying to put one over on us, and our faces turned suspicious.

"Now, that's as true as the day is long, I tell ya. Them ice worms is little fellers, about as small as a snap of thread. Drop a few of 'em in your glass of whiskey, and they'll keep you good and warm."

We gulped.

"No, kids, it warn't no bed of roses."

"You can sure as heck say that again, Homer," Grandpa Virgil said again. But as far as we remember, Grandpa Homer didn't.

"So did they struck gold?" we asked.

"Reports are fuzzy, ain't they, Virgil?" Grandpa Homer asked.

"Fuzzier than a bunny, Homer."

"But it does seem that the Wymore party eventually struck a nugget or two," Grandpa Homer went on. "It also seems that this Gottfried Schuh was made to do more and more of the work while everyone else sat in the saloons talking to the pretty dance-hall ladies. And so at some point, he must have told 'em to skin their own skunks,[4] and he stuck a few of them yellow rocks in his pocket and left those fellas up there and made his way back to Wymore."

"What happened to them?" we wanted to know.

Grandpa Homer looked at Grandpa Virgil. "Virgil, you got the dibs on that one?"

"Well, now, Homer. Lemme think . . . If I ain't mistaken, they went and became Eskimos, got into the igloo-making business, and turned a modest fortune."

"That sounds about right, Virgil," said Grandpa Homer. "But getting back to Gottfried Schuh now. He arrived back here in town a fairly wealthy individual and paid two

. . . .

4 Grandpa Homer and Grandpa Virgil always say that when they mean for somebody to do their own work.

barbers to shave off his beard. They had to use garden shears on it on account of his beard was so thick and wiry and full of stuff that normally don't belong in any man's beard."

"Were you the ones who cut it?" we asked.

That got a good laugh out of them both.

"No, it warn't us. And not our pas, neither. But it was our grandpas, and that's a fact, ain't it, Virgil?"

And Grandpa Virgil said, "Ain't no fact facter."

That was how we learned that Grandpa Homer and Grandpa Virgil were third-generation barbers, which explains how come they were so good at barbering. They always had just the right bowl to fit over our heads, and never once did they snip our earlobes.

"Now, where was we, Virgil?"

"Homer, you just brought Gottfried back to town."

"I did, indeed," said Grandpa Homer. "So now, Gottfried first got hisself some new clothes, since his was all full of seam squirrels.[5] Then he built a house of his very own and became a much-regarded fellow in town with bushy sideburns."

. . . .

5   Seam squirrels are lice. Ick!

"How I do remember them sideburns, Homer," said Grandpa Virgil. "All us kids had a good time laughing at 'em."

"So you can remember him?" we asked.

"Just them sideburns," said Grandpa Virgil. "What about you, Homer?"

"Course I do. But let me finish my story now. You see, kids, in spite of his nice house and them nice whiskers, Gottfried still had one problem. And you know what that problem was?"

We didn't.

"His problem was his feet."

"His feet?" we asked.

And Grandpa Virgil asked, "His feet?"

Grandpa Homer gave him a look and said, "That's right, Virgil, his feet."

And then Grandpa Virgil said, "Of course! How could I go and forget his feet like that?"

"I don't know," said Grandpa Homer. "Because, kids, when Gottfried was out in the Alaska winter diggin' for gold, his toes turned all black and just about nearly froze clean off."

"Froze *off?*" The story was really starting to get good!

"Well, they didn't froze off, but they did stay black as coal, and ever after that Gottfried had a problem finding shoes that didn't pinch his toes none. So you know what he done?"

We didn't, but we sure wanted to.

"Well, what he did was he used some of that gold he had left and built hisself a brick building and started manufacturing his own shoes."

"Manu-whatering?" we asked. Back then that was a long and complicated word for us.

"Shoe factory," Grandpa Homer explained. "Gottfried Schuh's Shoe Shop it was called. His business took off like a bottle rocket, and his piggies couldn't have been happier.

"Gottfried Schuh loved to tinker around in his shop. He came up with the darnedest things, and there warn't never a contraption he didn't like. And one day he caught wind of something called a McKay machine that made shoes all by its own. And he decided he just had to have hisself one of 'em, and four months later it arrived by train right at our very own train station.

"Well, he tested it out, and that thing spit out shoes for him left and right, but Gottfried didn't feel it lived up to his high standards of perfection. And so what he done is he improved upon it. And in time Gottfried got it so improved upon that he created the perfect shoe that never wore out. He called them Gottfried Schuh's Everlasting Shoes. If you've ever taken a good look at them black things Grandpa Milton[6] wears on his feet, then you'll know what Gottfried Schuh's Everlasting Shoes is. Them shoes Grandpa Milton wears is one hundred years old or more and got wore by Grandpa Milton's grandpa and Grandpa Milton's pa and now by Grandpa Milton hisself, and not even the shoelaces ain't never needed replacin'."

"How true, Homer," said Grandpa Virgil. "Not even a single shoelace."[7]

Grandpa Homer continued. "And soon word spread about them Everlasting Shoes. Folks took to calling them Gottfrieds, and folks came from all across the county and sometimes from clear out of state just to buy a pair. They'd

. . . .

6 You remember him. He used to be Mr. Snuggerud. He was Wymore's mailman back when Wymore had a post office, and you can still see him walking his old route every morning.

7 Today, knowing what we know from *The Handy Cyclopedia of Things Worth Knowing,* we'd call them robust and rugged.

stay in town right at the Any Hotel, where we all live today. Except for back then it was still called the Stanley."[8]

"How I do remember, Homer," said Grandpa Virgil. "I was only about knee-high back then, but I remember my pa sayin' how much hair there was in that hotel on any given day. Must've been good business."

"Must've been, Virgil," said Grandpa Homer. "But now listen close, kids, because here's what happened next. Within a month or two, there warn't a man, woman, or child within seventy-five miles of Wymore that ain't bought and wore a pair of Gottfrieds. And so Gottfried Schuh naturally started makin' more and more of his

· ·

8   It must have been lots of folks who stayed. We've seen hundreds of names carved into the floorboards or the windowsills or the window frames or the wood legs of our beds or just about anyplace in the hotel where there's wood for carving into. Grandpa Homer and Grandpa Virgil told us those are some of the people who came to Wymore back then to buy Gottfrieds. And the funny thing is that outside of their names, they all carved the same exact thing without a single exception we've been able to find, and we've looked everywhere. Here's just a few of the ones from our room: "Cager was here," and "Briney was here," and "Quill was here," and "Becky was here," and "Dyer was here," and "Ham was here," and "Hepsie was here," and "Obed was here," and "Jed was here," and "Clemmie was here," and "Kit was here," and "Mattie was here," and "Hy was here," and "Dot was here," and "Flossy was here," and "Nettie was here," and even "Zubia was here." Who in their right mind would name their kid Zubia?

famous shoes. After all, they was sellin' like blowout patches.[9] But the problem was his shoes ain't never wore out, and so no one ever needed to buy another pair of his shoes again. They just took to tradin' 'em with their neighbors whenever their feet growed some. And that's how come Gottfried Schuh never sold another pair of his Gottfrieds, and at the end of six months he went clean out of business with a huge pile of Gottfrieds in his factory."

Not only was that the bad part of the story, but it was also the part where our grandpas decided to spin us around in the chairs to face the big mirror, put a bowl on our heads, and give us a trim.[10] We usually felt sorry for ourselves when that happened, but as long as we got to find out what happened to Gottfried Schuh, we said we wouldn't do no complaining. Our grandpas said it was a deal.

"So there he was, kids," Grandpa Homer began again. "Penniless once more on account of makin' all them eternal shoes. But a man like Gottfried Schuh warn't a man to give up so easy. He might've been outta work and down on his luck and without a penny in his pants, but there

9 That's another way to call hotcakes.
10 Grandpa Homer could still see some back then, so it wasn't as dangerous as you might think.

was something he had on his hands. And can either of you guess what that was?"

We looked at each other in the mirror, and by the way our tongues were sticking out the sides of our mouths, we could tell each of us was trying to come up with a better guess. But none of us did, and so we just said, "Nope."

Grandpa Homer turned to Grandpa Virgil. "Virgil, what about you?"

And Grandpa Virgil said, "Why, Homer, I'd say he had his hands on the McKay machine, is what I'd say."

"Right you are," said Grandpa Homer. "The McKay machine. But what do you do with a McKay machine when you already got more shoes than you can ever find feet for in the whole state?"

That was another question we didn't know the answer to.

"Well," Grandpa Homer said, "if your name's Gottfried Schuh, you roll up them sleeves of yours and tinker around with that McKay machine and make it do something else useful. And you probably wanna know just what that was."

We did.

"Well, then, I'll tell ya," said Grandpa Homer. "But to tell ya, I'm gonna have to tell ya somethin' else first. You see, Gottfried still kept in contact with a sister he had back in the old country. They'd send letters to each other back and forth, and that was how Gottfried kept up on the gossip in his old village. Things like who had the best apricot preserves that season and whose hen laid the most eggs."

"Whose?" we asked.

"Whose?" said Grandpa Homer.

"Yeah, whose?" asked Grandpa Virgil.

Grandpa Homer just shook his head. "That ain't so important right now. But what is important is that sometimes his sister would write him of other news she heard about. Things going on elsewhere in the country. And one piece of news was about a new kinda machine that you could sit on and make go from point A to point B without you having to do none of the work. Kinda like a horse. Only it was a machine. You get what I'm gettin' at?"

This time we said we did.

"Good. Because when Gottfried read about that idea, he thought it sounded kinda nifty. Because remember, here's a man walked all over Alaska, freezin' his toes black. So if he could contrive up some sorta somethin' that would allow him to sit on his backside while this somethin' did all the work and brought him to where he wanted it to take him, wouldn't that sound good to you, too?"

We told him it would.

"Well, there you go. Gottfried Schuh got to work on his McKay machine, and took out the motor, and added some nuts and bolts, and put on a gear here and a belt there, and plopped that whole new engine on the front of a three-wheeled horse wagon. Then he slapped a horn to the front of it for safety purposes, and you kids ain't never gonna guess what he had hisself."

We could see in the mirror that both him and Grandpa Virgil were getting pretty excited, and we figured it had to be the big moment of the story. And so we just took a stab at it and said, "You mean a hippomobile?"

Well, our guess surprised them more than a four-cornered egg. In fact, we clean knocked them speechless, something that had probably never happened to those linguisters before.

It took them a minute to get their tongues back. And when they did, Grandpa Virgil said, "Them kids are as smart as new paint, Homer."

Chapter Seven:

"Let Me Call You Sweetheart"

SO NOW YOU KNOW that the word "hippomobile" we saw in the letter ain't got anything to do with the hippo you see in the zoo. It just means an old-fashioned car that looks more like a horse-drawn carriage. But what we still wanted to know was how come Gottfried Schuh gave it a name like "hippomobile."

"Good question, kids," said Grandpa Homer.

"Well, what's the answer?" we asked.

"Ain't no one knows," said Grandpa Homer. "Does they, Virgil?"

"Ain't nobody I knows who knows," said Grandpa Virgil.

"Theories abound, though," said Grandpa Homer.

"What are theories?" we asked.

"Theories? Well, them are like guesses. Ain't they, Virgil?"

"I'd call 'em guesses, Homer."

Then they went on to tell us some of the theories. One theory was that Gottfried called it a hippomobile on account of its gigantic size because the horse carriage he picked out for it was a mighty big one. Another theory was that his English just never got no good and he thought he was calling it something else altogether. The problem with this theory is that it didn't explain what he thought he was really calling it. Then there was the theory put forth by the librarian Grandma Henrietta. She said that in one of her dictionaries hippo means "horse" in a language called Greek. So according to her, Gottfried Schuh called it a hippomobile because it was made out of a horse wagon.

That made a light bulb turn on in our heads, but then Grandpa Homer asked, "Why in the world would hippo mean 'horse' in any language?"

That sounded like a good question to us, but we didn't know the answer and shrugged our shoulders. We were in kindergarten, after all, and didn't even know there was any other language outside of the one we talked.

Even Grandpa Virgil nodded his head and said, "Point well took, Homer."

And Grandpa Homer said, "I'm at the conclusion that why Gottfried Schuh called it a hippomobile is just gonna remain one of them mysteries of nature."

Since we both liked mysteries and thought nature wasn't too bad, neither, we asked, "So what ever happened to this mystery of nature?"

"Why, it's still in the old shoe factory down on Hill Street,"[1] Grandpa Homer said.

"It is?" That news floored us more than the wood planks beneath our feet.

"Maybe we should take 'em there right now, Homer. Whaddaya think of that idea?" asked Grandpa Virgil.

And we shouted, "Take us, take us!"

And so it was settled.

We'd never been all the way to Hill Street before, and so walking all the way down there, as Grandpa Homer and Grandpa Virgil were proposing, was a right big adventure for us, and we were as excited as jumping beans. But we'd hardly even gotten off the square when Grandpa Homer and Grandpa Virgil started in with their singing.

Now, don't mistake us; we enjoy a lot of them songs of theirs. Even back then, we knew several by heart and were glad to sing right along with them. But the song they picked for our hike down to Hill Street was so full of "sweethearts" and soft words and sentimental thoughts that we almost

. . . .

1 Even though everything in and around Wymore is as flat as old soda pop, it seems like every town's got a street called Hill Street in it somewhere. When people were naming the streets around Wymore, they noticed that if you placed a marble down on this one road, it would start to budge all on its own and roll a few inches. So they called that street Hill Street. At least that's what we've been told.

wished we hadn't said we wanted to see the hippomobile in the first place. And here's just two lines from that song so you know we ain't exaggerating none:

Let me call you "Sweetheart," I'm in love with you.
Let me hear you whisper that you love me too.

And the worse thing about it was that them lines were the refrain part of the song that they came back to over and over again like a dog to its dish. But we just stuck our fingers in our ears and hiked on like troupers. Soon, though, we turned a corner, and that lifted our spirits. We looked up at the rusty street sign hanging there crooked and read HILL STREET on it and knew we couldn't be far off now. And smack-dab there at the end of the street was an old brick building sitting there all by itself and surrounded by nothing but weeds.

We took off running and had time to inspect it before our grandpas got there. It was all closed up tighter than a secret, and the windows were too high to look through even when we jumped. We soon found a loose brick no higher than our chins on the side of the building. We tried to pull it out, and when that didn't work, we got a stick and shoved it in and heard the brick hit the ground on the other side. We peeked in, kinda like looking through a hole in a circus tent, but we didn't see no trapeze and no elephants, neither. In fact, it was too dark in there to see anything at all.

"Well, you two coming or ain't ya?" Grandpa Homer asked. We jumped out of our skin because there he was, standing right behind us.

We followed him around front, and there was Grandpa Virgil waiting with a giant key that looked to us more like a knucklebone. But he used it to unlock the door, and when he did, the door squeaked louder than a fiddle.

We let our grandpas go in first because it was mighty dark and cobwebby, and there was no telling what was lurking in there. We kept awful close to the doorway, at least until our eyes adjusted so we could see better. And once they did, we still didn't see no trapeze and elephants. But we saw something, all right. It was big and black and huge and went almost all the way up to the ceiling. It didn't remind us of anything we'd ever seen before, and we'll admit that we took a step closer to each other.

But it didn't seem to bother Grandpa Homer none. He went right up to it and took hold of a piece of it. Then he tossed it at us, and we caught it before we even had a chance to scream and jump out of the way. And it's a good thing we didn't scream and jump, because alls it was, was a shoe.

"That's one of them Gottfrieds we was telling you about," Grandpa Homer said.

"Them are all the shoes he never sold," Grandpa Virgil said. "Poor feller."

There were hundreds of them, too. Thousands.

Then Grandpa Homer and Grandpa Virgil took us around the corner into the back room. The windows weren't so dusty back there, so this time we could see right away what we were standing in front of. It looked like a giant horse carriage on three big wood wheels, and the wheels were as tall as us. Up front we saw a big horn attached to it that looked like it could blow your ears off. There was a tall steering wheel that didn't look like it could ever do a driver any good, and it was sticking straight up in front of the bench where you drove at. All in all, it was a strange contraption, but it was also the coolest thing to play on we'd ever seen in our lives. We didn't even mess with asking and climbed right up it faster than a squirrel up a tree.

The horn just coughed out dust and didn't work none, and the steering wheel was all stuck. But that just meant we had to make our own noises instead, and that had never been much of a problem for us.

We yelled, "Watch out, grandpas!" like we were heading straight for them. But it didn't seem like they even heard us.

Grandpa Homer was saying, "Ain't she somethin'?"

Grandpa Virgil said, "A real beaut, Homer. A real beaut."

"The pride of Wymore back when we was kids."

"Don't I know it, Homer. Don't I know it."

Then Grandpa Homer and Grandpa Virgil pulled out their hankies and blowed their noses so loud, we thought the horn was working after all.

"Would be somethin' to see her run again," Grandpa Virgil said.

"You can say that again," said Grandpa Homer.

But Grandpa Virgil didn't have a chance to, because we said it first.

No telling how long we stayed there playing on the hippomobile and how long Grandpa Homer and Grandpa Virgil stood down there reminiscing. That's what you call it when old people talk about the olden days and wipe their eyes and blow their noses.

We ended up having such a good time that on our walk back into town when Grandpa Homer and Grandpa Virgil decided to sing their song again, we even sung right along with them.

Chapter Eight:

Empty as a Cookie Jar

NOW, IT AIN'T LIKE we never saw the hippomobile again after that first day. Once we grew up another
notch on the wall, Mom agreed we were finally old enough
to go down there and play on it by ourselves. We'd found
out that playing on the hippomobile was just part of grow-
ing up here in Wymore. Pops told us he didn't do no different when he was our age, and even Mom had to admit
that she played on it once or twice when she was just a girl
in pigtails. The only problem was summer. Mom didn't
want us leaving the square when she was off working,
and Grandpa Virgil wouldn't give up that knucklebone
key for nothing in the world, not even for a barbershop
full of long-haired customers with long bushy beards. Like
Grandpa Homer sometimes says, life ain't always a bed of
roses.

That's why we were as excited as a hen house about that
letter we found in *The Cyclopedia of Things Worth Knowing*.
Because we was counting on it saying at least a little something about the hippomobile, and anything having to do
with the hippomobile always made our eyes see stars and

our hearts beat quick. Plus, we were sure as eggs is eggs that a few of our grandmas and grandpas would be interested right along with us. So we jumped right off Old Tom Wood to go and tell them. Stella scraped her prayer bones[1] some upon landing, but that didn't matter. And when Jimmy landed, he said, "Ow!" but that didn't seem to matter none at the time, neither. We just both brushed ourselves off and raised a good deal of dust on our way back over to Mabel's.

Now, by that time of day, you could usually find our grandpas and grandmas out and about in town. Grandma Winnie would be zooming around town in her golf cart at five miles an hour, and Grandma Pearl would be walking back and forth on the square in her safari suit, swinging her metal detector in front of her. Grandpa Chester was usually sitting on the bench outside Mabel's with a transistor radio pressed to his ear, listening to a ball game, and Grandpa Bert swept the sidewalk in front of his haberdashery at least three times a day, so you were bound to see him. The same went for Grandma Elsie, who was always tending her daisies out front of her flower shop. But that day when we turned the corner, the town

· ·

1 Them's her knees.

looked as empty as a cookie jar. The wind had picked up, and dust was swirling around on the street corners like little twisters. That's all we saw, and that was too bad, because we were ready to shout out our discovery to everybody.

So we ran over to Mabel's, and once we got the screen door open, we stumbled on through like tumbleweeds, ready to reveal our big surprise. But we noticed straight off that something was wrong. Sitting there at a table in the middle of the café was Grandma Mabel and Grandma Ida, and they never sat down on the job like that. Our other grandmas and grandpas were sitting around them like in a football huddle, and the TV weatherman report was turned off. In fact, the silence in the café ran so high it filled the cracks in the ceiling, and all the faces in there were as long as a rainy day. The only thing moving was the little fan up front on the lunch counter, rotating back and forth and making the pages of a menu flutter a bit in the breeze.

Even so, our excitement was popping out of us like a cork, and we couldn't help but shout, "Look what we found!"

But nobody so much as raised an eyebrow.

Chapter Nine:

That Old Wymore Smell

LATER THAT NIGHT WE were up in our beds, studying our long list of presidents. We couldn't concentrate, though, and were really just waiting for Mom to call us like she did every night at dot nine o'clock and not a single second thereafter. Nine o'clock was right before we went to bed[1] and right before Mom went to work. That graveyard shift of hers always sounded spooky to us, no matter how many times she said it wasn't really a graveyard. Alls it was, was just a huge warehouse with conveyor belts that transported gazillions of packages. It was Mom's job to stand there all night and sort them out. It didn't sound like a bed of roses to us, but Mom didn't complain none.

"Let's try it again, Jimmy James."

"I ain't in the mood, Stella."

"I didn't ask you your mood. George Washington."

"John Adams."

"Thomas Jefferson."

. . . .

1 Or at least when we were supposed to go to bed.

"..."

"I'm waitin'."

"Did you say Thomas Jefferson?"

"I did."

"I was afraid of that."

"Don't you remember who comes next?"

"Not exactly."

"Me, neither. But at least we're up to three now."

We stuck our lists back on our bulletin board and stared at the clock some more.

Our hotel room only has one phone in it. When it rings and we both wanna talk, we have to share, so we often bump heads as we try to hear what Mom's saying. She usually just says the same old stuff, like asking us if we brushed our teeth, even the ones way in the back, and if we combed our hair, and if we talked to our plates before meals,[2] and if we were eating enough. Mom wouldn't be Mom if she wasn't worrying about something.

That night everything was so different, though, that Mom didn't even get around to asking none of her questions. We picked up the phone in the middle of the first ring and banged our heads together like two pool balls and

. . . .

2 That's her way of asking if we remembered to say grace.

shouted, "Mabel's is closing!" without even saying howdy or nothing. That's what all the long faces were all about earlier that day when we ran into the café like we had just discovered electricity.[3]

We ain't ever gonna forget that moment, neither. The way our grandmas and grandpas just turned their heads and stared at us or didn't even bother turning their heads at all and just sat there stirring their cups of joe[4] or chewing on timber[5] or twirling a red checker on the table like Grandpa Milton was, or how Grandma Ida was twisting her dishrag around one of her fingers and Grandma Mabel was sitting there like a statue with her chef hat off.

We could tell something was wrong—we just didn't know what. We thought it might have something to do with the weather report. So we walked over quiet to our booth and slid on in and put *The Handy Cyclopedia of Things Worth Knowing*[6] down next to the napkin dispenser and the greasy bottles of ketchup and mustard and the bottle of relish none of us ever touched. We were still antsy

· ·

3 Ben Franklin did that, and we could always remember his name. But unlucky for us, we're pretty sure he wasn't a president.
4 A cup of joe is a funny way our grandparents have for calling coffee.
5 Which is just toothpicks.
6 We had put the letter back in it for safekeeping.

as a picnic but sat there all the same, just twiddling our thumbs and swatting at a fly that must've snuck its way in through the back kitchen door.[7]

We were glad when Grandma Ida finally got up off her chair and walked over our way. We couldn't wait to tell her the news. But it turned out she had news for us instead. She said, "You better order somethin' real good because you ain't gonna have many chances left."

That was strange talk coming from her. And we noticed she wasn't cracking her gum like usual. That made us suspicious as a sheriff. "Whaddaya mean by that, Grandma Ida?" we asked.

And Grandma Ida said, "Mabel's is closing, kids. Come the end of summer."

That was all she said, too, because her jaw started to quiver and her nose started to twitch and then tears rolled down her cheeks, just like always happened whenever she served a dish with raw onions.

And we said, "Mabel's is *what?*" Because she might just as well have told us that snow was in the forecast or one of our grandpas had grown a ponytail.

. . . .

7 Grandma Mabel kept it open to get the kitchen heat out because it was right hot and steamy back there, and that's how come Grandma Mabel's face was always red and drippy.

She took the dishrag off her shoulder and blew her nose in it and stuffed it in her apron pocket and sat down at our booth and talked turkey to us. And the only thing we were able to say the whole time was, "Yeah, but . . ." Like when she said that Mabel's just didn't do enough business, we said, "Yeah, but . . ." And when she said that it ain't no use and that they'd seen this day coming from miles away, we said, "Yeah, but . . ." The only time we didn't say "Yeah, but . . ." was when she left to go get us each a belch water[8] and a bucket of mud.[9]

Nine hours later, up in our room and in our PJs, we still couldn't believe it. Then the phone sprang to life and it was Mom calling.

"Mabel's is closing!" we shouted.

And Mom said, "I know."

"What? How could you know? You're not even here."

And that's how we found out that she and Pops knew, and everybody in Wymore knew, and they all had been

. . . .

8 That's water with all the bubbles in it that come back up your throat and make you have to belch a lot. Grandma Ida meant that as a big treat for us because we weren't allowed to just go belching whenever we felt like it. And now here we were getting belch water and no longer felt like belching.

9 That was another big treat, a bowl of chocolate ice cream.

discussing the matter for quite some time without ever bothering to tell us.

Well, that didn't sit square with us, and so we asked, "Why didn't you tell us nothing, Mom?"

"Anything," Mom corrected us. Then she said, "We didn't want to worry you about things you have no control over."

No control over . . . ? Well, we'd show her! Though at the time, alls we managed to say was, "Yeah, but . . . Where we gonna eat, then?"

That was when things turned serious and grave and made us feel that "serious and grave" should've been in that list of good diction in *The Handy Cyclopedia of Things Worth Knowing.*

Because Mom said, "In McFall."

And we said, "McFall? Is Mr. Buzzard gonna be driving us to McFall three times a day just so we can get our grub?"

And Mom said, "Well, no . . ."

"Then how are we gonna get there? By boat?"

Mom finally spit out the bone. "We'll just have to move there, is how."

Well, that was the straw that busted the hayloft. There was no way we were gonna move away from Wymore and Mabel's and Old Tom Wood and our room at the Any Hotel and the roof up on top and all the dust down in the square. And so instead of saying, "Yeah, but . . . ," we found some dogged determination and said, "You can pack up and move to your big city if you want to, but we sure ain't!"

We thought we had her good and cornered because we knew how hard it was for her to be away from us even for the summer. But she just up and laughed. *Laughed!* And she didn't even say nothing about us saying "ain't." Instead she called us what she always called us when she thought we were being cute. "Honey pies," she said, "how about we talk about this tomorrow? I have to go to work now."

That's where our conversation stopped at. We didn't even get a chance to tell her about *The Handy Cyclopedia of Things Worth Knowing* and the letter about the hippo-mobile we'd found stuck in the book. Mom sent us a good-night kiss over the phone, and we sent her one back, even though we didn't feel much like it. But we were a little afraid that we might not sleep so good if we didn't.

So we hung up the phone, and it was just the two of us again alone in Room #10. We didn't give a care about presidents no more, that's for sure. In fact, we were so thunder-struck that we didn't say nothing else at all. We just hit the light switch and climbed up into our beds. It would've been a good night to take our sleeping bags and go sleep up out on the roof, but now we didn't feel like enjoying nothing. Anyway, you needed a key to get up on the roof, and it was already too late to go ask Grandpa Bert up in Room #33 for it. He kept it on a string around his neck.

On any normal night, we'd both of us drop right off into a deep slumber after a day of getting wore out playing in the hot summer sun. But that night there was so much fidgeting going on in our beds that it sounded like the box springs were performing a concert. And then one of us coughed and the other one of us sneezed. Finally the burden of bad news got so great that we broke the silence.

"Jimmy James?"

"Yeah, Stella?"

"You awake?"

"Might be. You?"

"Yeah. I think I might be too."

We got out of our beds and tiptoed over to the window and tried not to step on the floorboards that made the loudest creaks. They creaked so loud that our grandparents in the other rooms would hear them, and then they'd know we were up and about and they'd tap on the wall with their walking sticks to tell us to get back to bed.[10]

. . . .

10 It isn't always easy having so many grandparents.

But that night we made it to the window silent as a prayer and knelt down at it and put our noses up to the screen. It had an old dusty air smell to it that we loved. It smelled just like Wymore itself. And believe us when we say that there ain't no rose ever smelled that good to us.

It was already as dark as a frown outside. The square was almost all dark, on account of that only one streetlamp still worked anymore. All the June bugs in town congregated there, even though it was July. We watched them bouncing off the light and listened to the cicadas making their music, and for a while we didn't say nothing to each other. We both knew what we were thinking, and what we were thinking about was the place we called home and that we sure didn't wanna leave it for nothing in the world. Thoughts like them are best for thinking and are a lot harder to talk about using real words, even if you're just talking to your twin. And so when we did finally say something, it was about all kinds of other stuff just to avoid talking about what we really wanted to be talking about.

"Jimmy James?"

"Yeah, Stella?"

"Can I ask you something?"

"Go ahead."

"Um . . . What state you think Pops is driving through right now?"

"You know I ain't no good in geometry."

"You mean geology?"

"Yeah, geology."

"Jimmy James?"

"Yeah, Stella?"

"Um . . . You think it'll be hot tomorrow?"

"I reckon."

"Say, what are you doin' with your mouth the whole time?"

"Wigglin' my tooth."

"You got a wiggler? I didn't think we had none left."

"Wouldn't be wigglin' it if I didn't."

"And you ain't told me?"

"Just happened today. When we jumped off Old Tom Wood and I banged it."

"Which one is it?"

"This one right here."

"Well, yank it and stick it under your pillow."

"That's what I'm tryin'. But it ain't comin' out."

"Gimme a try, then."

But for all the wiggling we did on it, it was stuck in there like a corn in a cob. We wanted to put it under Jimmy's pillow and see how much we'd get for it,[11] but we could tell we wasn't gonna get it out with our fingers.

"Wasn't there a chapter in *The Cyclopedia of Things Worth Knowing* with tricks on how to pull a tooth?"

"I think you're right, Jimmy James."

That rose our spirits an inch, and we agreed we'd look it up the next morning. But before we got back into bed, we took one more big deep smell out of the window screen.

"Jimmy James?"

"Yeah, Stella?"

"I ain't leavin' Wymore."

"If you ain't leavin', I sure ain't leavin'."

"Then we're gonna have to figure out a way to stay, ain't we?"

"Maybe we can say I gotta go to the dentist."

"That ain't no good, Jimmy James."

"Why not?"

"There ain't no dentist in Wymore."

"What's your idea, then?"

"I ain't got one yet. But if we use some dogged determination I bet we can think one up."

. . . .

11 We say "we" because the Tooth Fairy gave us both a little something when one of us lost an ivory.

Chapter Ten:
Looking for Something to Look At

WANTING TO FIGURE OUT a way to stay in Wymore sounded good the night before, but when you wake up the next day and it's morning and the sun's shining you in the eyes and giving you the sun grins,[1] and you're down in the middle of the town square kicking dust around, and you don't see nothing but closed stores and empty buildings and rusty cars all around you, then it don't look so easy as it sounds.

We'd just come out of Mabel's after each having a Battle Creek in a bowl,[2] and Jimmy was chomping on a carrot because Secret Trick #1 in *The Handy Cyclopedia of Things Worth Knowing* on how to work out a loose tooth was by biting into something hard. The suggestions the book gave was a carrot, a radish, a turnip, a beet, and something called a rutabaga. With choices like that, that's how come Jimmy picked a carrot. Grandma Ida was a bit surprised

. . . .

1   Them is the funny faces you make when you stand facing the sun.
2   Alls that is, is cornflakes.

to hear he wanted one, but she didn't ask us no questions, and we didn't feel like offering any explanations. We were just in one of them moods for having a secret that only us and the Tooth Fairy knew about.

"That carrot doing you any good?"

"Naw. You want it?"

"No thanks. My teeth ain't wiggly."

Jimmy stuffed it in his back pocket, and we spent some time throwing pebbles at the old broke-down cars and trying to figure a plan to stay in Wymore.

"Stella?"

"Yeah, Jimmy James?"

"You know how Mom's got heightophobia, right?"

"You mean acrophobia?"

"Yeah."

"So what?"

"Well, why don't we say we got McFallophobia?"

"They ain't gonna buy that, Jimmy James."

"How about traffic lightophobia?"

"They ain't gonna buy that even less."

"Well, at least I'm sayin' somethin'."

After a while, we decided to go up onto the roof of the Any Hotel because that's where we sometimes got our good ideas at.[3] We walked over to get the key from Grandpa Bert, who like usual was out sweeping the sidewalk with his wood broom. We almost couldn't see him on account of all the dust he was whirling up.

"Good morning, Grandpa Bert," we said.

He stopped his chores and leaned on his broom and shaded his eyes and looked up at the sky and said, "Looks like it's gonna be another scorcher." Which was how people in Wymore often greeted each other, instead of just saying plain-old "Howdy!"

Just to be nice, we inquired about the forecast[4] before asking for the key to the roof.

"Just don't stay up there too long. You'll dry out like raisins on a day like this."

We said we wasn't gonna, and Grandpa Bert started taking the key off from around his neck. Before he handed it over, he asked us, "First name me the first five presidents."

So word was out about our homework, but lucky for us we now knew the first three good as our back pocket. While we were getting dressed that morning, we'd discovered that

· ·

3 Like the time we had the idea to collect ants, or the time we had the idea to set a world record in sneezing by putting pepper in our noses.

4 Grandpa Bert said we was in store for more triple digits.

president number four and president number five both had the same first name, but we didn't remember what it was.

"I do believe James is the name you're lookin' for," Grandpa Bert said.

Jimmy smacked hisself on the forehead and said, "Oh, yeah, James."

Then Grandpa Bert gave us the key along with two gumdrops.

"Thanks, Grandpa Bert!" And off we ran toward the Any before he asked us for the next five presidents.

When you walk into the lobby of the hotel, you'll find yourself in the coolest spot in all of Wymore. It's dark in there and has a tall ceiling, and the floor and walls are all made out of real marble. There ain't no better place to rest your cheek against on a hot day. We've been told that a long time ago there were people in uniforms and little red caps standing behind the reception desk just waiting to take care of you and carry your bags up to your room. And there was one guy whose only job was to run the elevator. That's right, our hotel even has an elevator, even though it ain't never worked since we've been alive. It looks like a small metal cage, and it's all locked up now, and it probably didn't play elevator music like elevators do today.[5]

To go up, you gotta take the steps, and when you start walking up, it keeps getting hotter each step you take. The hallways are all dark and narrow, and the long strip of carpet laying there is as wore out as an old song. The wallpaper is peeling off worse than summer skin, and there's a smidgen of spookiness about everything, even for us at the age of ten. So to get to the roof, we always run up faster than Moody's goose and don't stop until we're on the top floor and in front of the door we gotta unlock. It ain't always easy to stick the key in the keyhole when you're jittering, but once we get it unlocked, we bust on through the door like wind through a tunnel and find ourselves on the roof and back in the light of day.

That's where we were now, high up above the town of

· ·

5   We know this for a fact because we were in one once in McFall last
    year when our class went on a field trip across the street from our
    school to the courthouse. All fourth-graders get to go, and the most
    exciting thing about it is that elevator. Not only does it got music; it's
    also got mirrors and carpeting and makes your stomach drop to your
    knees when it takes off. The courtroom was boring in comparison to
    that because alls it had was uncomfortable wood benches, and you
    weren't even allowed to talk.

Wymore. All the other buildings are only two stories, and so from the hotel roof you can see clear over them and straight out of town and all the way until the sky meets the prairie grass. The view is what some of our grandpas and grandmas call sublime beauty. We'd always just shrug our shoulders when they said something like that, but now that Mom was talking about leaving Wymore, we kinda understood what they were getting at.

We parked our biscuits on the rickety old table up there,[6] hoping it would hold us for another day, and stuck them gumdrops in our mouths and gazed down at the town square and set our minds to brainstorming. We kept right at it real hard and didn't let up none for what felt like an hour and must've been at least three minutes.

"Got any ideas yet, Jimmy James?"

"Uh-uh. You?"

"Not yet."

Another at least two minutes went by.

"How 'bout now, Jimmy James?"

"Nope. You?"

"Uh-uh."

And after one more minute, we had another conference.

. . . .

6 Where our grandpas used to go and play cards and smoke cigars at.

"Jimmy James?"

"Don't ask."

It just wasn't no use. Maybe you've noticed that too, how that you can't have a good brainstorm when you need it most. Alls we were getting for our efforts was dry goozles.[7] Plus our moods were turning worse than a burnt pot of whistleberries.[8] So it suited us just fine when we saw some commotion down in the square that took our minds off our problem.

Our grandpas were beginning to congregate in front of Grandpa Frank's old furniture store, and that could only mean one thing.

"Must be Train Day coming up, Jimmy James."

"Sure looks that way, Stella."

Now Train Day, you need to know, is the one day a week a coal train runs through town. It doesn't stop none—a train ain't stopped here in more than fifty years. But everybody gathers at the old train station to watch it pass by and hear it blow its whistle. And there warn't almost nothing in the world we wouldn't have liked more than to be able to ride on it someday.

. . . .

7   Your goozle is your throat.
8   Them is beans, and Grandma Mabel knew how to make even the
    lowly and humble bean into something rare and exquisite.

Seeing that not much else ever goes on in Wymore, Train Day constitutes a true town highlight, maybe even its truest, and everybody makes the most of it. Just picture twenty-eight grandmas all with trucker hats that say I ♥ TRAINS and matching shirts that have KEEP ON CHUGGIN' written across the front.[9] The grandmas are responsible for organizing the picnic and decorating the station with streamers and making sure everybody has a little flag to hold and wave as the train goes by.

Our grandpas are in charge of hauling all the tables and chairs over to the train station.[10] And that's why they were there in front of the furniture store that morning, chewing on their timber and waiting for Grandpa Frank to show up and unlock his store.

"Here he comes now!" someone said.

And sure enough, Grandpa Frank was running up the street and putting on his second shoe and fastening his suspenders all at the same time. That was just like him because he was always late.

· ·

9 They used to make us wear a hat and a shirt too, until we told them we were getting too old for stuff like that.

10 We asked them once why they didn't just leave everything set up over there, and they told us because it ain't never been done that way and that tradition was tradition.

"Lying around too long on the mule's breakfast again, was you?"[11] we heard one of our grandpas ask.

"My alarm clock must not be workin'," Grandpa Frank answered.

Our other grandpas pulled the pieces of timber out of their mouths and made a big show of throwing them on the ground.

"It ain't been workin' since February 2, 1974, Frank," said Grandpa Chester.

"I know, I know," Grandpa Frank said. "Time to think about replacin' the battery."

Then he pulled out a key chain with more keys on it than a barn has flies. Somehow he found the right one on the first try and unlocked the door to his store, and all our grandpas filed in one after the other just like schoolchildren.

"Sure would be neat if the coal train broke down here in town one day," one of us would always say when Train Day came. "Then we could at least climb up and take a look at it."

"Would be as neat as a pin. But you know it ain't gonna happen."

. . . .

11 The mule's breakfast means "bed" on account of that a mule's breakfast is hay and hay used to be what mattresses were made of.

We had to settle for the next best thing to riding the rails—standing there each week and counting the boxcars and hoppers as they rumbled by louder than buffalo. The most we'd ever counted was 132 of them, and that was just last summer.

Soon enough our grandpas came back out of the furniture store. They were pulling and dragging and tugging old armchairs and rickety rockers and busted recliners and lopsided benches and three-footed ottomans and warped dining tables. And that wasn't even the hard part. Then they had to lift and hoist and boost and rear everything up onto their golf carts so they could drive it over to the train station two blocks south. Most times they left a trail of furniture behind them like bread crumbs through a forest. It was enough to make you bust your gut laughing. We also got to hear some good old-fashioned cursing, but we won't be including any of that here.

Anyhow, there we were, watching preparations for Train Day get under way and wiping sweat off our foreheads and swinging our feet, and sometimes Jimmy would give his tooth a wiggle. In other words, nothing special was going on. And yet it was at that moment when we were least expecting it that we got the brainstorm we'd gone up to the roof looking for. It went something like this:

"Jimmy James?"

"Ahgrhruallla?"[12]

"Ain't it kinda funny?"

"Ain't what kinda funny?"

"Goin' through all this trouble just to watch a loud, dirty freight train go by?"

"I don't think so."

"Why not?"

"Shoot, Stella. People are always lookin' for something to look at."

"Like how do you mean?"

"Like remember what our teacher said about Paris? How everybody's always going there just to take a picture of the Evil Tower?"

"*Eiffel*, Jimmy James. Rhymes with 'rifle.'"

"That could be, Stella. And what about that Leaning Tower of Pizza in Italy? Remember learning about that one?"

"Nope."

"You don't?"

"I remember learning about the Leaning Tower of *Pisa*, Jimmy James. But I guess you're right."

. . . .

12 Which is what "Yeah, Stella?" sounded like when Jimmy tried to talk and wiggle at the same time.

"Course I am. Like Pops says, 'Ain't no use being wrong.'"

We went on back to doing nothing for a while, but then suddenly all four of our eyes got wide and sparkly as silver dollars, and we both said, "That's it!"

We knew right away what each of us was thinking. If everybody's always going all the way to Paris or to Italy just to look at some tower, why shouldn't at least some of them come to Wymore instead? First off, it's closer. Second off, there ain't no lines. And third off, ain't no one ever had their picture taken standing next to a hippomobile before.

Alls we figured we needed to do was to dust it off some, give it a squirt of oil, and get it up and running again.

Chapter Eleven:

Confounded

Onions

WE BEE-LINED IT STRAIGHT to Mabel's and direct into our booth. Grandma Ida must've saw our sweaty faces and read our minds because before we could even catch our breath, she said, "Two dog soups with hail, coming right up!" That may sound yucky, but it's really just ice water.

We were still breathing hard when she came and put down our drinks square in front of us. "Thanks, Grandma Ida," we said, and started making the slurpy sounds that quench your thirst the best.

"Looks like you two have a fire to put out," she said.

"We do," we said, soon as we came up for air. "We're gonna save Mabel's!"

Grandma Ida stopped chewing her gum. "Come again, now?"

And we said, "You better go get Grandma Mabel for this."

She hurried off and got her from the kitchen, and they both sat down across from us, and we said, "Listen close, 'cause here's our plan." Then we talked about Paris, and we told them a thing or two about Italy, and we were careful to mention how tourists are always looking for a good place to eat. That perked up their ears, all right. And that's when we hit them with the hippomobile.

Grandma Ida sat there the whole time wiping little spots off the tabletop with her dishrag, like that made her concentrate more. Grandma Mabel wasn't moving a muscle. She kept her arms rested on the table. They were red from cooking and thick like logs, and we were always mesmerized by the blue anchor she had tattooed on her left forearm. And whereas Grandma Ida sometimes said, "Uh-huh" and "I see" and "All right," Grandma Mabel remained silent as a fish.

After we finished talking, Grandma Ida wasn't chewing her gum, and that worried us a bit. But it was Grandma Mabel's reaction that threw us like a horseshoe. She was known to be tough as nails, and even though she still hadn't moved none, we saw she was crying so hard, it almost looked like she was making a pot of tear soup.

Grandma Ida said, "Mabel," and put an arm around her.

But Grandma Mabel just said, "It's them confounded onions I was choppin'." She got up and stomped back heavy through the swinging kitchen doors without another word.

We waited until them doors finished swinging, and then we leaned in over the table and asked Grandma Ida real quiet, "Did we say somethin' wrong?"

Grandma Ida just smiled and said, "Not at all, kids. In fact, I think you said somethin' right. Because if you ask me, it ain't such a bad idea you got there."

That made us smile wide as a rainbow.

"Except for one thing."

Our rainbows disappeared. "What's that?" we asked.

And Grandma Ida answered, "The hippomobile ain't never run in my lifetime. And as far as I know, not in any of your other grandparents' lifetimes, neither."

"That ain't what Grandpa Homer and Grandpa Virgil told us once," we said.

"You know better than to believe everything comin' outta them mouths of theirs."

That gave us a bad case of the slumps, all right.

But then she said, "Of course, far as I know the Eiffel Tower don't run none, neither."

That's when we remembered the letter and took it out of *The Handy Cyclopedia of Things Worth Knowing*. "Maybe this here could help us some," we said.

Grandma Ida looked over the envelope a moment before pulling out the letter. She unfolded it and looked at it some in one direction, then turned it upside down and looked at it some in the other direction. "Where'd you get this here letter?"

"Found it yesterday stuck in this book."

"You did, did ya?" Grandma Ida asked, and went back to sizing up that piece of paper awful close. She seemed to have something on her mind because we could just about hear the gears in her brain going *click* and *clank*.

Finally she said, "You know what? I think we better run this by Henrietta. She's the one person around here who just might be able to read this thing. Because if I ain't mistaken, it looks like it's from Gottfried Schuh."

Chapter Twelve:

 Dingsbums

WE AIN'T SURE HOW popular checkers is anymore outside of Wymore, but Grandma Henrietta and Grandpa Milton played it nearly every day. As far as we can remember, Grandpa Milton never won a single match. He calls that perseverance. But if you asked us, that ain't the word we would've used.[1]

By the time the three of us got over to their table, Grandma Henrietta was grinning like a shark and rubbing her hands together so you would've thought she was trying to start a campfire. Grandpa Milton had that fiddle-faced look he always got when he was about to lose. "It ain't over till it's over," he said.

We had a hard time disagreeing with that, but not Grandma Henrietta. "It's over now, Milton," she said, and she took her newly crowned king and zigzagged it clean across the board so fast, it near made us dizzy. And by the time we could see straight again, every last one of Grandpa Milton's pieces had disappeared.

· ·

1   "Hopeless" was the word that came to our minds.

"Gotcha again, Milt!"

Grandpa Milton sat there a moment staring at all his checkers piled up next to Grandma Henrietta and then called for a rematch.

"Kids," she said to us, "your Grandpa Milton's a glutton for punishment."

"Glutton nothin'. I wanna be red this time," said Grandpa Milton.

Someday you've just gotta hear Grandpa Milton talk. Because his voice is as deep as a well. We think that's because he's gotta be the tallest person you're ever gonna see without the use of binoculars.

"The color ain't got a thing to do with it," Grandma Henrietta said. "It's all in the fingertips."

We didn't want them starting another game, at least not until Grandma Henrietta looked at our letter. We asked if we could show her something.

"It's all right by me. I'm gettin' kinda tired of winnin', anyhow," she said, and let out a fake yawn. "What do you say, Milton? Ain't you gettin' kinda tired of losin'? I know I would be."

Grandpa Milton flashed us a wink. "Kids, when I was growin' up, I was always learned how you was supposed to give old ladies a break." His deep voice made the table vibrate and the remaining red checkers dance on top of the board. Then he stood up—and kept right on standing up—and said, "But I'll be back, Henrietta." And in less than three large steps, he was out the door.

"So what'cha got for me?" Grandma Henrietta asked us.

"It's the kids who came across an interesting item, Henrietta," said Grandma Ida, and gave us a nod.

So we pulled out the letter and handed it to Grandma Henrietta and watched her squint at it and move it closer up and then farther away and then closer up again. "This here's from Gottfried Schuh," she said.

"What'd I tell ya?" Grandma Ida said to us, and we told her thanks and gave her a hug that squeezed the air clean out of her.

"Where'd you two find this old document?" Grandma Henrietta asked us.

"In an old book," we told her.

"What old book would that be?"

We held it up in front of us like at show-and-tell.

Grandma Henrietta leaned forward, squinted, and then took the book right out of our hands. First she said nothing and just ran her hand soft over the cover. "Ah, yes, *The Handy Cyclopedia of Things Worth Knowing*." Then she leaned back, let out a sigh, and rested her eyes. "If it was going to be in a book, it'd have to be this one."

"How come is that?" we asked, but didn't get an answer. Grandma Henrietta just went right on resting her eyes. So we finally coughed some and asked again.

Her eyes popped open and she said, "Because the *Handy Cyclopedia* was the very first book the Wymore library ever did own. After the Bible, of course. It was a big sensation back in the day, I do recall, and there probably wasn't nobody in town who didn't come in to consult it at some time or other, whether to find a cure for itchy feet or just to read a poem by Shakespeare. When this letter came back, someone must've decided to use it as a bookmark."

Grandma Henrietta then dug around in her purse and pulled out her Ping-Pong paddle case. It wasn't really a Ping-Pong paddle case—that's just what we called it because it looked like one. What was in there was her magnifying glass. Grandma Henrietta couldn't read much without it, and she always told us that being a librarian had its own special occupational hazards.[2]

"Grandma Ida said you could read it," we said.

. . . .

2 Grandma Henrietta said them included things like squinty eyes, paper cuts, and nightmares about the Dewey decimal system.

"Is that so?"

"Now, don't play shy, Henrietta," said Grandma Ida.

"My German's rusty as an old gate, but I sure can try," she said.

Grandma Henrietta aimed her magnifying glass at the old letter she had flattened out on the table, and we stared over her shoulder. The small letters looked as big as hopper legs[3] now.

Meine liebe Schwester Magda!
Von Herzen freue ich mich . . .

Of course, we couldn't make heads, necks, or tails out of it, but we hoped Grandma Henrietta could. Sometimes she nodded her head and sometimes she bit her lip and sometimes she itched her chin and sometimes she whispered German words to herself that didn't mean beans to us.[4] Then for a while she didn't do anything at all, and we were afraid she might be asleep.

"Grandma Henrietta?" we asked.

. . . .

3   Hopper as in grasshopper.
4   When we asked her what she was saying, she just said, "Hold your potato!"

Then she lowered her magnifying glass and said, "Ach, Gottfried!"

"What's it say?"

"It's a letter from Gottfried to his sister Magda. Seems she was about to marry a fellow named Heinrich Sonnenschein, and Gottfried was writing to say he would be coming to the wedding. And from what I can make out, he drops several hints that he's mighty interested in Heinrich's sister. Says right here how his heart aches every time he thinks of Kunigunde."

"Cooneygunda?" What kind of a name was that?

"So he asks his sister if Kunigunde's hand was still available. And if she thinks Kunigunde would be interested in coming back to America with him."

We didn't care much about Kunigunde's hand. "Yeah, but don't it say something in there about the hippomobile?"

"Sure does," Grandma Henrietta said.

Grandma Ida nodded to us and said, "Go ahead and tell her."

So we told Grandma Henrietta all about our plan to save Mabel's, and even though she laughed some at our comparison between Paris and Wymore, she thought our scheme wasn't without promise.

"You just might be onto something," she said. "Because Gottfried writes here how he'd just invented some kinda newfangled dingsbums for his hippomobile and . . ."

"'Dingsbums'? What's a 'dingsbums'?" we asked.

"Oh, that ain't nothing but a German word for 'thingamajig.' And, anyway, he writes how it's this dingsbums of his that now starts the motor."

"So that means it'll work!" we shouted. And Grandma Ida gave us a smile.

But then Grandma Henrietta said, "Well, he says here how he was gonna remove that dingsbums before he traveled back to his sister's wedding."

"Remove it?! Why'd he do that for?"

"Says he's worried that when he ain't here, other folks in town might wanna take his vehicle out for a spin. And he didn't want anyone wrecking it."

"You mean that without that dingsbums thingamabob, the hippomobile ain't gonna work?"

"I ain't sure, kids. I'm no mechanic. But listen to this: he writes here that he was gonna put the dingsbums in his house for safekeeping. So that if anything happened to him on his voyage back home, his sister could send somebody back out here to claim it. Seems he thought he had a gold mine with that hippomobile of his. Maybe he was plannin' on makin' as many of them as he did Gottfrieds. Who knows? It's all pretty amazin', ain't it?"

Amazin'? We didn't think so. Because who knew where in the heck that dingsbums was now? And if we didn't have that piece, how were we gonna get the hippomobile up and running? And if we couldn't get the hippomobile up and running, then what?

"Save your poutin' for a rainy day," Grandma Henrietta said. Then she turned around in her chair. "Homer, Virgil, get your buns over here! I got some questions for you."

They got up from their table, and Grandpa Virgil took Grandpa Homer by the elbow and led him across the café and sat him down in a chair and then sat down himself.

Grandma Henrietta said, "Listen, either of you old farts know what ever happened to Gottfried Schuh?"

Grandpa Homer said, "Gottfried Schuh?"

And Grandpa Virgil said the same thing Grandpa Homer said. "Gottfried Schuh?"

And so Grandma Henrietta said, "Is there an echo in here?"

"Well, now, lemme think," said Grandpa Homer. "He was that odd German fellow, wasn't he, Virgil?"

"Sure is a long time back, Homer," said Grandpa Virgil.

And they sat there a moment shaking their heads slow and rubbing their jaws hard and squinting like they had grit in their eyes.

Meanwhile Grandma Henrietta rolled hers. "I'm waitin'."

And so was we.

"Virgil?" said Grandpa Homer.

"Yes, Homer?" said Grandpa Virgil.

"You happen to remember somethin' about a weddin'?"

"A weddin', you say?"

"Yeah, you know. Man and wife. People throw rice at 'em."

Alls Grandma Henrietta could do was shake her head. "These two boys love nothin' more than to hear theirselves talk."

"I may be blind, but I heard that," said Grandpa Homer.

And Grandma Henrietta said, "Good. Think about it sometime. But first answer me my question."

"That's just what I'm tryin' to do if you'd keep quiet," Grandpa Homer said. "You're awful loud for a librarian, you know that?"

But then Grandpa Virgil said, "Now that you say

weddin', I do think I recall a matter of a weddin', Homer. Didn't Gottfried return to his homeland on account of a relative of his gettin' married?"

Grandma Henrietta gave us a big nod. "A *Schwester*, maybe?"

All of us said, "'*Schwester*'?"

And Grandma Henrietta said, "Sister."

"I think you might be right, Henrietta," said Grandpa Homer. "For a change."

And Grandpa Virgil said, "Now, Homer, don't start . . ."

"Forget it, Virgil. Ain't no use tryin' to teach an old mutt new tricks," said Grandma Henrietta. "Just tell me what happened to him."

"What happened to him?" asked Grandpa Homer.

"That's what I said," answered Grandma Henrietta. "What happened to him."

"Well, shoot . . ." Homer shook his head. "Virgil?"

"Far as I can recall being told, he just left one day and ain't never come back. I remember people sayin' how they went in his house months later and found a half-ate piece a sausage lyin' right smack on the middle of his kitchen table."

"That rings a bell, Virgil. 'Older than a Gottfried sausage.' Ain't that what people always used to say?"

"My, my," said Grandpa Virgil. "Older than a Gottfried sausage . . . Them sure was the days, Homer."

"Boys!" said Grandma Henrietta. "Snap out of it!"

That did the trick. Grandpa Homer said, "Say, Virgil, didn't he send a letter back here from Germany one day?"

"I ain't sure, Homer. Maybe he did. But maybe he didn't. But maybe he did. I guess I ain't sure."

"Wasn't there some talk in it about him himself getting married?" Grandpa Homer asked.

"Why, Homer, that's startin' to sound familiar, I do think."

"Now we're gettin' somewheres," said Grandma Henrietta.

"To some girl with a funny name, if I reckon right," said Grandpa Homer.

"Why, indeed, Homer! Now that you say a funny name. Because I ain't never forgot a funny name when I hear one," said Grandpa Virgil. "But I just can't seem to remember what it was . . ."

"Wasn't it somethin' like Esmeralda?"

"Esmeralda? No, that don't sound right. Brunhilde?"

"Kriemhilde, maybe, but not Brunhilde. Was it Kriemhilde, Virgil?"

"Giselinde?"

"Gundelinde? Was it Gundelinde, Virgil?"

"Did you say Gundelinde?"

"That's what I'm saying, Virgil."

"I think that might've been it, Homer. Gundelinde . . . Yup, I think maybe. No forgettin' a doozy like that, that's for darn sure."

"How about Kunigunde, boys?" asked Grandma Henri-etta. "You think maybe that—"

But she didn't have time to even finish her sentence because Grandpa Homer and Grandpa Virgil both shouted, "Kunigunde! That's her!"

"Never forget a doozy like that, that's for darn sure, Homer," said Grandpa Virgil.

Then Grandma Henrietta asked, "So is you two sayin' that Gottfried Schuh left Wymore to go to his *Schwester*'s —I mean, his sister's—wedding and then ain't never re-turned back to Wymore because he hitched his wagon to a pretty little star named Kunigunde? Is that what you two is sayin'?"

Grandpa Virgil looked at Grandpa Homer. "Is that what we're saying, Homer?"

"We wasn't but little kids at the time, but that's what I always heard. Ain't it, Virgil?"

"I reckon so, Homer."

"Thank you, boys. You've been a great help," said Grandma Henrietta. "For a change."

"Always a pleasure doin' business with you, Henrietta," said Grandpa Homer. "But tell me, what are you interested in Gottfried Schuh for all of a sudden?"

"Later, Homer," Grandma Henrietta said, and turned to us. "You kids get it, don'tcha?"

The looks on our faces must've told her we didn't.

"Then listen close," she said. "Because accordin' to this letter you found, before Gottfried traveled back to witness the marriage of Magda Schuh and Heinrich Sonnenschein, he was gonna take somethin' he called a dingsbums out of his hippomobile. That way ain't no one could drive it while he was gone. And now accordin' to these two old fogies, Gottfried really did go to that wedding just like he wrote he was gonna. But it seems he got married himself to one Kunigunde Sonnenschein, and for reasons ain't no one knows, Gottfried never returned back to Wymore. You followin'?"

We were.

"Good," said Grandma Henrietta. "Now hold on to your britches. Because if he really did take that dingsbums out of the hippomobile and left it at his house like he said he was gonna, that means it could very well still be there."

Well, that was the most dramatic and sensational news we'd heard all summer. Because it meant if we could just find that dingsbums, we could make the hippomobile run again. And if we could make that happen, people from all over would wanna come and look at it. And if people came from all over to look at it—well, you get the idea.

Just then Grandpa Milton returned. He sat himself down into a chair and placed a book on the table called *How to Win at Checkers*. It had more dog-ears in it than a kennel. And he said, "Did I hear you talking about Gott-fried Schuh's old house?" And once again the checkers began doing a dance.

And Grandma Henrietta said, "That's correct, Milt. You know where it is?" Because if anybody was gonna know, it was gonna be him on account of that he used to be the Wymore mailman.

"I do," Grandpa Milton said, "But it ain't nothing but big bluestem now."[5]

We knew what he meant by that. "Gone?" we asked.

"With the wind," Grandpa Milton replied. And he

- -

5 Big bluestem's a tall grass you see all around these parts. People also call it turkey foot because it branches out at the top to look like a turkey foot. But if you don't know what a turkey foot looks like, we can't help you much.

puffed his cheeks out and made like wind was blowing, and the sound that came out was like a long, low train whistle, and our hair even blew back some.

What Grandpa Milton was getting at was that Gottfried Schuh's house had since broken down, fallen apart, and got taken back over by nature. It was happening all the time to the houses off the square on account of how they were just made out of wood. Some of the brick buildings on the square were going that way too, if a little bit slower.

"What'cha got the frownies for?" Grandpa Milton asked.

And we said, "Because we were hopin' to find something at his house."

Grandpa Milton said, "Well, I'm sorry to bring you bad news like that. It's just like back when I was a mailman. One day I was bringin' a birthday card; the next day it was the gas bill."

Grandma Ida snapped her fingers. "Now, wait a second, folks. Just because his house ain't there no more, that don't mean the dingsbums ain't."

And Grandpa Homer said, "Would someone finally like to tell us what's going on here?"

And Grandpa Virgil said, "I second that, Homer."

But Grandma Ida went right on talking. "I reckon

there's a chance that dingsbums you're lookin' for might still be there in the topsoil somewheres. Just waitin' to be dug up by a couple of kids right about your age."

That was all we needed to hear. We had Grandpa Milton explain to us right fast where Gottfried's house used to be.

As we were making to leave, he said to Grandma Henrietta, "Now, about that rematch."

And Grandma Henrietta said, "Oh, Milton, ain't you never gonna learn?"

And Grandpa Homer said, "Can someone please fill me in here?"

Chapter Thirteen:

How to Yank a Doorknob

SINCE WE WERE GOING digging, we first had to stop at the old hardware store to pick up some tools. It used to be called Pickler's and now was called Ickler's.[1] Everyone went there to borrow whatever it was you needed so long as you brought it back soon as you were done with it. However, there wasn't much left in there now, and nothing that you could plug in and make a lot of noise with. Most of the shelves were empty except for the dust mice, but we were still hopeful about finding what we needed.

We pushed open the door, and the bell over it went *clank* instead of *ding*. We walked up and down the aisles grabbing whatever we thought might come in handy. If we hadn't found that wheelbarrow to put it all in, we don't know what we would've done. Here's just a sample of the things we took: a sprinkler, half a saw, an old jar of peanut butter that we couldn't get the lid off of, a shovel that was

· ·

1   You can probably figure out how come.

taller than we were, a bucket with a hole at the bottom, a bent screwdriver, one of them small claw-looking things for digging weeds with, a rusty chain about as long as a belt, a straw hat, a step stool, a light bulb we busted before we even got to where we were going, a faucet, and two paintbrushes, one for each of us.

Once we figured the wheelbarrow was heavy enough, we steered back for the door, and that's when Jimmy grabbed a ball of string.

"How's that gonna help us dig up a dingsbums, Jimmy James?"

"It ain't for diggin'. It's to pull out my tooth with!"

Secret Trick #2 on how to yank a tooth was the door trick. You tied one end of a string around your tooth and the other end around a doorknob. And on the count of three, you were supposed to slam that door shut so that it pulled your tooth clean out of your mouth in one fell swoop.

"You sure you wanna go through with this, Jimmy James?"

"Just make sure you double-knot your end."

Once we were all knotted up, we counted with our fingers and then we slammed the door good and loud. The bell went *clank*, but ain't nothing else happened.

"Take two steps back, Jimmy James, and I'll try it again."

And sure enough, this time something did get yanked. Except for it was the doorknob and not the tooth.

So we gave up and let the tooth stay put. We each took one handle of the wheelbarrow and pushed it out the door and walked down the street where our grandmas and grandpas were going about their everyday business.[2] And as we passed them by, they each gave us a funny look and asked us what in the name of Joseph we were up to.[3] We just told them, "Go ask Grandpa Homer. He'll tell ya."

We pushed and took a right at the corner where the old Stop sign was laying flat on its face and left the square behind us and pushed our way down Water Street. That was the street with the giant water tower on it that was the tallest structure in town. The name WYMORE was printed on it in thick black letters, but on account of all the sun and the

- -

2   As usual, Grandpa Bert was sweeping, Grandpa Chester was listening to a ball game, and Grandma Pearl was searching for pennies, bobby pins, and bottle caps.

3   This Joseph fellow got mentioned every now and then, but we ain't sure who he was exactly.

wind and the grit, the name was all faded out and looked more like WYMORE.[4]

By the time we got to the next corner, our arms were already aching, and we were still only at Baker Street. We know Baker Street good as the man in the moon because that's where we used to live at back when we were little kids. Our old house has done seen its better days, though. The front porch is sagging like a belly after a good Sunday meal, and the steps leading up to it are all rotted out like teeth. The front door is so wobbly, it could be blown in by the first wolf that comes around, and the windows are all busted out like black eyes. Most of the paint's chipped off, too, and up on the roof there's a hole where the chimney must've been.

"Kinda good to be livin' at the Any, ain't it?"

"Sure is, Jimmy James."

We each picked up our side of the wheelbarrow and marched onward. According to Grandpa Milton's

---

4   Pops has promised us that as soon as we turn twelve, he'll climb up there with us. Although when Mom heard that, her reaction was, "Like heck you will!" And she brought down her iron on the ironing board so hard that a whole cloud of steam shot out of it and rose clear up to the ceiling.

directions, we still had several blocks to go, and we ain't exaggerating when we say that somehow the blocks were getting longer and longer the farther we walked on them, like they was stretching like taffy. So we tried swapping wheelbarrow sides, and we tried walking backwards, and we even traded off wearing the straw hat, but the wheelbarrow got heavier no matter what we did. By the time we reached the fork in the road we were scouting for, both of us had blisters on our hands the size of baked beans.

But we didn't stop, and soon the blacktop ran out and we hit dirt gravel. Grandpa Milton told us to keep a lookout for a rusty mailbox on our left. Said we couldn't miss it on account of that the red flag would be sticking up. And true to his word, we spotted the mailbox from far off and were happier than clams.

But soon as we got there and put down the wheelbarrow, we blew on our hands and looked around and saw what we were up against. Short of that mailbox, there wasn't anything out there except for weeds, weeds, and more weeds. There wasn't even no sign as to where exactly Gottfried's house could've stood at. There wasn't a gate, and there wasn't a porch, and there wasn't a hole in the roof on account of that there wasn't no roof. It was just like Grandpa Milton said. Nothing but wind and bluestem.

"Now what are we gonna do?"

"I was gonna ask you the same thing."

We pulled the shovel out of the wheelbarrow, and we took the bucket and walked our way through the weeds. We were hoping we'd still maybe find a portion of Gottfried's house in there, like maybe a step or a patch of floor or even a nightstand without a bed next to it. But the only thing in them weeds was all the hoppers we were scaring up. And they jumped on our shoulders, and they clung to our shirts, and a few of them got comfy up in our hair.

We finally stopped looking and just picked what we thought was a good spot to start digging at. But it didn't take us long to determine that the dirt was harder than a day-old dinner roll. The shovel busted clean off soon as it broke ground, and we were left standing there holding the handle. So we got down on our knees, but by the time we managed to dig out our first real dirt clod, we were as wore out as a welcome mat.

"Jimmy James?"

"Yeah, Stella?"

"This ain't no use."

"Nope. It sure ain't."

Chapter Fourteen:
Lady
Metal

WE WERE AS EXHAUSTED as a tailpipe that night and couldn't hardly wait any longer for dot nine o'clock. We'd already sprinkled some water on our faces and licked down our hair and wrestled our way into our pajamas and were now sitting up on our beds. We had some time to spare, and we knew what we were supposed to be doing. The presidents were staring mean at us from up on the bulletin board. But we left them stuck there like donkey tails and wallowed some more in our misery instead.

We were mighty glad when the phone started ringing, and we jumped off our beds and picked it up and said, "Mom?"

And the voice on the line said, "Who you turkeys callin' Mom?"

"Pops!" we both shouted.

"Hey, now, go easy on my ear. I might need it again someday."

Pops didn't call us at regular times like Mom did because he was always on the road, and that's why it was always a special treat when he did call. We'd always wanna know how many states he'd trucked through since the last time we talked, and if he blew out a tire or not, and what kinda greasy spoons he'd ate at, and if his back pain was acting up on him again, and how much he was looking forward to a Mabel's blue-plate special.

But that night we had our own stories to tell for a change. We told him everything and more and did so all at once and at the same time and didn't bother with coming up for air until we got around to the very end of what we had to say and how we was gonna save Mabel's. And then we asked Pops, "So what's a dingsbums look like, anyway, huh?"

Pops said, "Quit your gobblin', the both of ya's. I ain't understood a lick of what you've been sayin'."

So we had to go back and repeat everything all over again from the very beginning. This time after we finished, alls Pops had to say was, "Jeez, my back's achin' me."

So we said, "Pops! Ain't you been listenin' to a thing we said? Mabel's is closin'!"

And Pops said, "Course I been. But what I don't get none is why you didn't get Grandma Pearl to help you out."

"What's Grandma Pearl got to do with anything?"

"Listen, I'll admit she can be a little funny-looking in

them safari suits she likes to wear. But that's just between you, me, and the fence post."

We told him mum was the word.

"However, I reckon that if you're ever gonna find a dingsbums down at Gottfried Schuh's old property, it sure ain't gonna be by diggin' with a sprinkler and a step stool."

"Then what should we be diggin' with?"

"Nuthin', that's what."

"Pops, you ain't helpin' none!"

Pops said, "Diggin' like that ain't gonna get you but a handful of blisters. But listen. I'm guessin' this dingsbums of his was probably nuthin' more than an early kind of electric spark plug is my guess. 'Cause that's what Gottfried was gonna need to jump his engine. You turkeys followin'?"

We said we were, even though we really weren't.

"Good. Now, you ain't so knuckleheaded as to think that a spark plug's made o' plastic, is you?"

"We ain't no knuckleheads!" we said.

And Pops said, "Good. That means you take after me."

"Pops, come on!"

"*You* come on. You know your Grandma Pearl is Wymore's Lady Metal."

And we shouted, "Her metal detector!"

"Vwah lah!"[1] Pops said. "You go back out there tomorrow with Grandma Pearl and see what you can find. I'll give you a buzz tomorrow night, and if you unearth a dingsbums, then we'll see about getting this plan of yours up and runnin'."

"You really think?" we asked.

"First you find, then I'll think," Pops answered.

That made us happier than a lizard in the sun.

Then Pops had to go and say, "And speakin' of thinkin', how are them presidents of yours comin' along?"

. . . .

1 One of them French words Pops liked to use. This one here means something like, "Bingo!" We ain't positive we're spelling it right.

Chapter Fifteen:
The Cat's Meow

THE NEXT MORNING THERE we were again, on our way back down to Gottfried Schuh's plot of weeds. This time we weren't pushing no wheelbarrow. In fact, we weren't even walking. Grandma Winnie had offered to take us down there herself on her golf cart.[1]

You never needed to twist Grandma Winnie's arm much to have her take you out for a ride. If she wasn't in Mabel's flipping through an old wrinkly copy of a car magazine, you could find her out tinkering on her golf cart in a pair of gray overalls that had her name stitched on them in red just like a real mechanic. Sometimes there'd be a smear of grease stretching across her forehead, though some of our grandmas and grandpas said she put that there just for looks. She also wore racing goggles and had red flames on the sides of her golf cart, but it didn't go no faster than honey dripping from a spoon.

· ·

1   Provided that we wore our bicycle helmets. It was a little
    embarrassing, but it was one of them rules made by Mom, and
    Grandma Winnie was a stickler when it came to rules.

Once we got on, Grandma Winnie said, "So, kids, let's lay some rubber!" And off we rolled, smooth, silent, and slow, to the other end of the square to pick up Grandma Pearl. She was easy to spot in her wide safari hat and that vest that had more pockets than we had fingers and toes. Plus, she was the only one standing on the corner holding a Pioneer 505 metal detector.

Earlier that morning at Mabel's over a plate of cluck and grunts,[2] we had talked to Grandma Pearl about helping us find something rare and exquisite. And before we even had a chance to explain, she held up her hand and said, "Say no more. Know all about it."

"You do?" we asked.

"Course I do."

"How'd you find out?"

"Take one guess."[3]

"Well, can you help us any?"

"Kids, I ain't never passed up the opportunity to find a dingsbums. Meet me at the corner of Main and Market in ten."

. . . .

2 Grandma Ida served us a big helping of eggs and bacon that morning.

3 Just by the way she said it, we could tell she meant Grandpa Homer and Grandpa Virgil.

So there we were, ten minutes later, scrunched in between Grandma Winnie in her racing goggles and Grandma Pearl in her safari hat. Back behind us where the golf clubs were supposed to go was the metal detector. That's what we wanted to talk all about, but Grandma Winnie and Grandma Pearl got to stirring the breeze[4] quite good without us. While they recalled weather events like the Giant Drought of '93 and the Huge Gales of '94 and the Blazing Sun of '95 and the Muggy Nights of '96, alls we could do was sit still and watch all the old, empty, and crumbling houses go by.

Once we finally got to Gottfried Schuh's property and the golf cart came to a complete stop, we tore off our helmets and jumped right off the back and yelled, "C'mon, Grandma Pearl, let's metal detect!"

That's when we got our first lesson on the subject. Grandma Pearl told us that true metal detectors didn't even call it metal detecting.

"Well, it ain't plastic detectin'," we said.

"Kids, it ain't called detectin' at all," Grandma Pearl informed us. "We experts call it prospecting."[5]

. . . .

4 That means they was gossiping.
5 We should probably mention at this time that Grandma Pearl was a paying member of the North American Prospectors Club.

"Prospecting? Ain't that what Gottfried Schuh did out in Alaska?" we asked.

"Indeed, he did," she said.

Well, that was the cat's meow! Because we'd had no idea we were gonna get to be just like Gottfried Schuh.

"Now, be so kind and help pull me to my feet," Grandma Pearl said. "My knee ain't what it used to be." So we each took one of her hands and tugged her up into a standing position, and once she got there, she was good as grits. "Now then, let's get to work," she said.

We followed her around to the back of the golf cart, where she put on a set of headphones that were bigger than cream-filled donuts. She plugged them into her Pioneer and turned it on, and the whole display panel lighted up like a Christmas tree. It had more buttons on it than a Sunday shirt, plus two knobs besides.[6] Grandma Pearl also concerned herself with "Ground Balance" and something called "No-Motion All-Metal Mode." She was an expert, all right.

Meanwhile we went and grabbed the supplies we'd left down there the day before. After some debating, we

. . . .

6 One was called the Sensitivity Knob and one was called the Notch Knob, but unfortunately we done since forgot what both of them did.

decided we'd be best off with that claw thing and the bent screwdriver. By the time we got back, Grandma Pearl was ready to go.

"Quiet, now, and follow me," she said. "And no talkin', neither."

Then off we went on our very own prospecting expedition. It was even better than we'd been hoping for. At least at first. We maybe weren't climbing up through snowy mountains, and we weren't sipping ice-worm cocktails, and we didn't get to have dirty beards and smell bad, but we were stalking through weeds that came up over our ears, and bugs and insects were buzzing all around us, and we had tools with us that we were hoping we could utilize real soon.

Grandma Pearl was in the lead, gently swinging her Pioneer 505 back and forth over the ground. Right behind her came Grandma Winnie, still wearing her racing goggles. Then right behind them was us.

We were willing and prepared to spend half the morning or more pacing slow up and down through the weeds in search of a dingsbums that no one quite knew what it would even look like. So we were knocked clean out of our socks when after no more than three minutes Grandma Pearl stopped walking and held her 505 over one and the same spot and consulted her display and announced, "I got somethin' here!"

Which was our clue to get to work. So we scrambled up front and got down on our prayer bones and started scraping furious at the ground right where the Pioneer was pointing at. Grandma Pearl had told us we'd never have to dig more than three or four inches, and we thought that three or four inches weren't nothing. And besides, we couldn't believe we'd already found it!

Except for two things. One was that three to four inches ain't as little as you think. And the other thing was that we hadn't found it. Alls it was, was a stinking old rusty nail.

"Crud!" we said.

And Grandma Winnie said, "Watch your mouths!"

"'Crud' ain't a bad word," we said.

"It's got four letters, don't it?" Grandma Winnie replied.

"That's all part of prospectin', kids," Grandma Pearl said. "You gotta learn to see the beauty in everything. That's a good lesson in life." She grabbed the nail from out of our hands and stuck it in one of them vest pockets. "I tag, record, and conserve everything I find," she said. She didn't even sound disappointed at all.

Well, a rusty nail might've toasted her bread all right, but not ours. And that was just the beginning, too. As the morning wore on, our enthusiasm for the prospecting life wore off. Here's just some of the worthless stuff we dug up: a nail, a tin can lid, a nail, a flattened-out bottle cap, a nail, some wire mesh, a screw, a nail, a small hoop,[7] a piece of wire, a nail, a nut, a washer, a spring, a nail, a nail, a bolt, a nail, a nail, a nail, a nail, a nail, and another cruddy nail.

Each time Grandma Pearl's Pioneer 505 beeped or buzzed, she gave us the word, and we came around and dropped down to the ground and started digging. Until finally we were close to telling her to dig it up herself if she wanted it so bad. But we knew that kind of mouthing off would get us grounded for the rest of the summer, and so we bit our tongues and just kept on digging, one nail after the next.

"I got something here," said Grandma Pearl for the gazillionth time. "Pretty strong signal, too." She sounded as focused and untired and excited as she had at the outset.

Whereas we thought, *Strong signal. How exciting!* But we got down and began to scrape and dig. Soon, at least, the

7   Grandma Pearl got pretty excited about that one.

tip of something came to light, and we rubbed at it a bit with our thumbs and got the dirt off and were relieved it wasn't another stupid nail. Then we dug and scraped a bit more and saw it wasn't a bottle cap, neither. Then we saw it wasn't a spring, and it wasn't a hoop, and it wasn't a washer. When we were finally able to pull it out of the earth, we gave it a solid rubdown and blew on it hard and placed it in the palm of our hands. Then we stood up, and Grandma Pearl and Grandma Winnie bent down, and all four of us stayed there like that just staring at this funny-looking piece of metal.

"You think this is it?" we asked.

Chapter Sixteen:
Now We're Thinkin'!

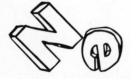

"YOU THINK THIS IS IT?"

That's what everybody was asking everybody else that whole afternoon at Mabel's. And then they'd go passing it around careful as caution from one palm to the next, with everyone getting a good look at it before handing it on. "You think this is it?"

And the whole thing was that ain't no one had a clue. Alls we did know was that it was an odd-looking critter, something like a cross between a caterpillar, a corkscrew, and a fishing hook. And we also knew that we ain't ever seen nothing like it before, neither. But that was about all we knew. That, and that Pops would be the only one who could supply us with a definitive answer, since Grandpa Buster, who used to own the auto parts store, was no longer with us. But Pops hadn't called yet, so everybody at Mabel's was left to speculating. We listened close to what our grandmas and grandpas had to say on the matter while we sat in our booth sucking on the double black cows[1]

. . . .

1   Those are double-thick chocolate shakes.

that Grandma Ida had been nice enough to supply us with.

"This really could be it."

"Heck, could be."

"It ain't no hairpin, that's for sure."

"Just think if that hippomobile gets up 'n' runnin' again."

"Sure would be somethin', wouldn't it?"

"Sure would."

"Heck, maybe it really could save Mabel's."

"Would be nice. Been eatin' here my livelong days, after all."

"Don't I knows it."

"Sure would hate to see Mabel's go."

"If Mabel's goes, so does Wymore."

"Can't let that happen."

"We just need more people comin' to town, is what we need."

"The more people come, the more people'll eat at Mabel's."

"We done know that much. That's what them kids was talkin' about yesterday."

"I guess they was, wasn't they?"

"Maybe we just wasn't listenin' that good."

"Well, then, listen now. 'Cause if we're fixin' the hip-pomobile, why not fix up Wymore with it?"

"Now we're thinkin'!"

"Don't know about you, but I been thinkin' for over seventy years now."

"I for one wouldn't mind takin' a wet rag to them clunkers out there. Put some shine back in 'em."

"I guess I could pump up a tire or two."

"And how about fixin' the sign up on the Any while we're at it? Have it spell out 'Stanley' again?"

"I still got the *T* somewheres."

"I got the *L*. Little rusty. But I gots it."

And so on and so on. They were getting so excited that they didn't even tell us not to slurp our black cows. All it had taken was some dogged determination and a little old dingsbums. If indeed that's what it was. We were still waiting impatient for Pops to call.

Then sudden as a rooster crow, the pay phone on the wall rang, and everyone at Mabel's hushed as though a preacher just stood up. We left our booth fast as jackrabbits and ran to the phone and climbed up on a chair and picked it up and said, "Mabel's Café. How may we help you?"

Chapter Seventeen:

The Scribbles on the Wall

"SO, YOU TURKEYS, what'd you find?"

"Well, we found somethin'," we said. "But it's pretty weird-lookin'."

"Weird? How weird?"

"Hold on," we said.

We asked for the dingsbums, and our grandparents started passing it down from one grandma and grandpa to the next like they were playing hot potato. Then it got to Grandma Ida, and she brought it over to us high on a tray like she was serving a black-and-blue[1] on a silver platter.

"Okay, we're lookin' at it," we told Pops.

"Then lay it on me."

We laid it on him best we could and told him what we thought it kinda resembled like.

And Pops just said back to us, "A cross between a caterpillar, a corkscrew, and a fishing hook? You sure about that?"

. . . .

1 That's a special kinda steak that's black on the outside but juicy on the inside.

"Well . . ."

So Pops put a number of questions to us, like how much we thought it weighed, and if it was heavier on one end than it was on the other, and what color it was, and if it looked like it was put together with different kinds of metal, and a host of other questions that didn't make no sense to us.

Finally Pops had to admit, "I can't be for sure if that's the dingsbums we're lookin' for or not."

That made our hearts sink like stones.

Pops must've heard them go *plop*, too, because he said, "Now, just hold on a sec."

So we held on and listened to Pops scratching his beard and making other thinking kinds of noises. And while he did that, we looked at all the stuff people'd scribbled there on the wall next to the phone over the years. There was lots of three-digit telephone numbers, and sometimes a name to go with it, like Cecilia or Harvey. And somebody wrote "By milk." There was also some hearts there too, with initials in them and an arrow going through. But what we liked most was the train times scribbled there, like "Arr. 8:04"[2] and "Arr. 2:37" and one in military time

. . . .

2   Arr. meant "arrival."

that said "Dep. 17:01."[3] And looking at them train times like that, all smeared and fading out, tickled our traveling bones something awful.

Pops pulled us back from our thoughts. "You turkeys still there?"

We said we were.

"Ain't tomorrow Train Day?" Pops asked.

And we said, "Yeah."

"Then, I tell you what. I'll do some callin' around and see if I can't get that train to stop in town and have the engineer pick up what you found and bring it on down the line to where Mr. Buzzard can pick it up. And then I'll ask Mr. Buzzard to deliver it out to Dixie's.[4] And from there a buddy of mine'll truck it out my way so I can have a good look-see at it with my own two eyes. And if I reckon it's the dingsbums we need to get that hippomobile on its feet again, then I'll see about making a pit stop through town so I can fix her up. How's that sound?"

And we said, "Better than a root beer float!"

Then Pops said, "Good deal."

We were about to hang up, but somehow that "Dep.

. . . .

3   And Dep. meant "departure."
4   That's the nearest truck stop to where we live.

17:01" was still gnawing on us hard. And so we said, "Hey, Pops?"

"Hey, what?"

"We've got even a better idea . . ."

Chapter Eighteen:
Train
Day

THE COAL TRAIN PASSED through town at exactly 9:54 a.m. unless it was late like always. From our window that morning, we saw our grandmas already bustling like bees back and forth across the square. They had tablecloths draped over their arms and were carrying trays topped with party hats and napkins folded into pyramids and arrows and cones and rosebuds and candlesticks.[1] Every week they somehow managed to decorate everything together in just the right way so as to make things look festive as fireworks.

We hurried and changed into our clothes and licked our hair down into place and rubbed the remaining sand out of our eyes and gave our teeth a good finger polish.[2] Then we grabbed our school bag that was waiting for us right by the door and left our room like we had wings.

Mabel's didn't serve food on Train Day since we all ate

. . . .

1   We tried to learn the art of napkin folding on many occasions, but the only shape we ever mastered was the crumpled-up ball.
2   There was no tooth wiggling on account of that we had more important business to attend to.

a picnic over at the train station. The café got turned over to whatever grandmas were in charge of the cooking that week, and that gave Grandma Mabel and Grandma Ida some well-deserved time off sitting on their backsides. Everybody agreed that it was the least we could do to repay them for the hard work they did for us all week long. However, we still stopped by Mabel's to pick up our birdseed[3] because even birdseed was something special on Train Day. It was always a whole tray of life preservers[4] spread out up on the lunch counter for you to pick and choose.

Mabel's was empty when we walked in, and the lights were off, and the chairs were all up on the tables. We guessed that meant ain't no one had started preparing the picnic food yet. You couldn't hear nothing but a fly or two against a windowpane. It always shivered us like a winter day to see Mabel's all deserted like that, and even more so that morning.

"If our plan doesn't work, Jimmy James, Mabel's is gonna look like this all the time."

"Mabel's and Wymore, too."

We didn't feel like spending any extra time in there.

. . . .

3   Otherwise known as breakfast.
4   Donuts!

We just went straight up to the counter and grabbed off our two life preservers. They were easy to spot because they were the ones covered in rainbow sprinkles and stuck on a stick. Then we returned back outside quicker than you can say "You betcha."

We caught up with Grandpa Homer and Grandpa Virgil, who were on their way over to the train station. Grandpa Homer was tapping along with his long white cane, and Grandpa Virgil had his box of teeth[5] strapped over his shoulder because him and Grandpa Homer were responsible for the day's musical entertainment. That always consisted of old barbershop standards and the traditional Wymore Train Day ballad they thought up all by themselves. Plus they had on those funny-looking singing hats we done described you about.

"You two must be right anxious," Grandpa Homer said.

And we told him we were.

"You ain't forgot the dingsbums, I hope," Grandpa Virgil said.

We showed him our school bag with the billy goat decal on it, which is our school mascot. "Right in here," we said. Inside our school bag was our school box, and inside

---

5   Also known as an accordion.

our school box was the dingsbums, or at least what we hoped was the dingsbums. We had it wrapped up in a little piece of sheepskin we once brought home from the state fair and which was the softest thing we owned.[6]

Our railroad station wasn't no Grand Central, that's for sure. It was just a one-story brick building that didn't look any different than any other brick building in Wymore. There wasn't a line of yellow cabs honking out in front, and there wasn't any fancy-looking people fighting to get in them. Alls there was, was some buffalo grass growing up through the cracks in the blacktop and switch grass sprouting high as the roof and attracting butterflies.

We walked around the building and were as struck as a lightning rod to find our grandmas already setting out the plates and bowls of vittles, seeing as how we'd just licked our donut sticks clean and stuck them in our back pockets. There was everything and more laid out on the tables because our grandmas always made sure there was something for everyone. We spotted corn on the cob piled

. . . .

6   We'd also like you to know that we collect those little banana and apple stickers that are stuck on every banana and apple you buy and that our school box was nearly all covered up with them. To be exact, we had forty-seven apple stickers and thirty-nine banana stickers, and that was just from the start of summer.

high as haystacks, and big bowls of steaming whistleberries accompanied by chunks of bacon, and tube steaks[7] floating like logs in hot water, and racks of first ladies[8] all smothered in homemade BBQ sauce, and leaning towers of hockey pucks,[9] and icebergs of potato salad, and giant pickles the size of submarines, and all sorts of other withits. Then there was fly cake[10] and Georgia pie[11] and Magoo.[12] Generally you could tell what we ate at Train Day just by looking at the stains on our shirts afterward.

"Why we eatin' so early?" we asked, and each nabbed a bacon bit out of the pot. The picnic usually didn't get under way until the train went by and Grandpa Homer and Grandpa Virgil had sung their ballad. That's just how the tradition was set up, and traditions die hard in places like Wymore.

And our grandmas told us, "'Cause you ain't gonna be here once the freight passes. Or did you forget?"

. . . .

7　Hot dogs.
8　Spare ribs.
9　Hamburgers well done, just like we like them best.
10　Which was actually just raisin cake. But from a distance you would've thought the raisins was bluebottles.
11　Peach pie.
12　That's custard pie, but we ain't got any idea how it came to have that name.

Forget? How could we have? Because that's what was making this Train Day even more special than normal. Remember when we told Pops we had an even better idea? Well, our idea wasn't just better—it was better than butter. We asked if instead of just handing off our school box to the train engineer and waving "oh revwah,"[13] why couldn't we hop on and ride with it for a spell?

And Pops said, "Ooh lah lah!"—which means something like "Oh, boy." And then he said, "We just better not tell Mom about this until you're back home."

And we said, "It's a deal!"

So that's why we were sitting down early to fill our shirts. One by one, our grandmas and grandpas joined us at the center table. But we didn't want to start grubbing until Grandpa Homer and Grandpa Virgil performed their Train Day ballad. Grandpa Virgil broke out his box of teeth, and him and Grandpa Homer took their seats at the edge of the long picnic bench, right where everybody could see them good. We all sat at attention while Grandpa Virgil pulled and squeezed his accordion and Grandpa Homer warbled with affection. And soon we all began singing along:

· ·

13 That's another French word Pops uses that we ain't sure how to spell. But we do know what it means: "goodbye."

Train Day comes each week at ten
Unless the train runs late.
Warn't never a town like Wymore is
That honors cargo freight.

Grandpa Virgil finished the song in a flourish of notes, and we clapped our hands sore. And that's when you could say the picnic got into full swing.

Everybody made long arms in every direction to get to the food they desired, and everyone was reaching so fast you would've thought we were gonna get tied up in one big arm knot. Once we all had a full plate, we picked up our pitchforks and saws and began filling our shirts, and for a time ain't no one spoke, and the only thing you heard was chewing, slurping, an occasional burp, and cutlery knocking against each other like a sword fight.

If we hadn't been departing after eating that day, we would've played washers[14] and I Spy and sardines, and then listened to Grandpa Virgil chatting a little more on his box of teeth and witnessed some good toe-smithing[15] on the part of our grandparents. But we *were* departing that day.

. . . .

14 A tossing game.
15 Toe-smithing means "dancing."

So what happened instead was that we heard the toot of a train whistle, and everybody jumped up from the table all at once. Our grandmas hurried over to us and brushed off our crumbs and tucked in our shirts and wiped the corners of our mouths and the bottoms of our chins and tidied us up all uncomfortable like we were going to church. Then we all stood there lined up straight as flagpoles two feet from the edge of the platform and waited eight more long minutes until we saw the lead locomotive come around the bend and then stop on a dime right smack in front of us. And the screeching it made to do so just about split our ears in two.

Chapter Nineteen:

Miles

HERE'S A QUESTION FOR YOU. How many times can twenty-eight grandmas tell you to be careful and to be good and to not misbehave and to pay attention and to listen to what the train engineer tells you and to be careful? Well, the answer is such a big number that you ain't gonna be able to pronounce it out until you're at least in high school.

But somehow we managed to break free from our grandmas. Our grandpas who were talking to the engineer stepped aside, and we climbed straight up these rungs welded onto the outside of the locomotive and climbed in through a door that if you ask us was awful small for such a huge train as the one we was now on.

"Howdy," said the man sitting there. Then he turned and aimed a stream of juice[1] straight into a coffee can down by his feet. We knew it went in because it rang out like rain tinkling on one of them rusty hubcaps laying in the square.

. . . .

1   Juice in the sense of tobackey.

"Hi," we said, and sorta held on to each other just in case the other one felt a bit scared.

"Call me Fitz," he said, and tipped his hat that said MILES on it. His hair was all matted down underneath in a way our Mom would never allow us to leave the Any Hotel with.

We didn't have the guts yet to tell him what he should call us, but then he smiled at us just standing there and showed us a mouth full of brown teeth, and so we smiled right back at him. Then he shook our hands so tight, we were certain we heard knuckles snap and our smiles turned into more of a grimace.

"Welcome to CNABTB!" Fitz said.

And we said, "Huh?"

And Fitz said, "Explain it to ya later.[2] Now you better lean out the window and wave to your folk. 'Cause we're outta here."

So we did like we were told, just like our grandmas and grandpas told us to do. The window was even tinier than the door was, and we could barely squeeze our two heads out of it. But when we did, we saw how high up we were

· ·

2 He did, too. He taught us how them letters stood for the names of what coal mine the train started out from and what destination it was headed for.

and that we must've been 15 feet up above the tracks. Mom would've undergone a fainting spell for sure.

Whatever our grandmas and grandpas were saying to us, we couldn't hear none of it on account of the locomotive noise. That was fine with us, since we figured it was the same stuff they'd already been telling us hundreds of times. So we just waved and saw our grandmas waving with their handkerchiefs, and our grandpas lifted their hats solemn off their heads.

Gradually and slowly they turned smaller and smaller, and then more parts of Wymore came into view. And we was like, "Hey, look, there's the Any!" and "There's the water tower!" And soon enough the whole town grew so small that we could cover it up first with our hand, then with our fist, and then with just our thumb. And then when we took our thumb away, the town was gone altogether, and we were officially on an adventure.

"Take a sit-down," Fitz told us.

There was a seat next to his, and when we sat on it, it was like sitting up on a throne, that's how big and cushy it was. It easily fit the two of us plus our school bag in the middle. That's when we looked out ahead of us through the windshield for the first time and saw the two long lines of rails we were traveling on. And the farther you looked at them, the closer and closer they got together, until way up ahead of you they turned into a single dot.

"Pretty amazin', ain't it?" Fitz said, like he knew what we were thinking.

We nodded our heads.

"So, I hear you's carryin' somethin' special in that school bag of yours."

We just stared down at it and maybe held it a little tighter. How did he know?

"Old gentleman at the station told me about it whiles you was being tended to by the ladies."

"Oh," we said. Which was only the third word we'd yet spit out, and they'd all been roughly that small.

"Said I'm to take you down to Maggie's Crossing. Hand you off to Mr. Buzzard."

"Yes, please," we managed to say.

"Yes, please," Fitz repeated, and slapped his leg and laughed like we said something funny. "You two kids are all right." Then he turned his head some and nailed that coffee can again.

We sat looking straight ahead without moving our heads a single notch.

"Maggie ain't gonna like that none, tell you that much."

We didn't ask him how come, but he told us, anyway.

"She don't like it none when a mile of coal sits there rumblin' on her land. Even been known to come out with a shotgun. Wearin' them big boots of hers stickin' out from under her skirt."

Our throats went dry. Why didn't Pops tell us nothing about Maggie? And nothing about Fitz? And we thought that we maybe should've asked Mom first.

"Still lives in a dugout, she does. You two know what a dugout is? And I ain't talkin' baseball."

Our eyes glanced over at him, but our heads didn't move none.

"It's like a little hut dug right into the side of hill. Nuthin' but a dirt floor and a potbelly stove. And yet they say she's sittin' on natural gas worth millions of dollars. You believe that?"

Our shoulders went up and down a little bit.

"Good ol' Maggie," Fitz said, and shook his head and laughed some more.

We asked each other what natural gas was and if it had something to do with what happens when you eat too many whistleberries.

"What you kids whisperin' over there?"

"Nothing," we said. But it turned out he heard us, anyway.

"Well, I ain't right sure exactly what natural gas is,

neither. Alls I know is it's fuel, like oil, and you can get it out of the ground."

"Oh," we said. Another big, long word.

"I tell you what. It's about time we had some fun here. Whaddaya say?"

We didn't say nothing, but it sounded good to us.

"You think you two is able to help ol' Fitz out some?"

We first looked at each other to make sure we thought it'd be okay. Then we said, "Yes." Slowly we were starting to warm to the situation.

"Good deal," he said. "Now, see that there post coming up down on your right. Gotta a black X on it?"

We did, indeed.

"Means we got a grade crossin' comin' up."

A grade crossing?

"Just means a road of some sort is gonna be crossin' the tracks. And when that happens, you know what we gotta do?"

We reckoned we did. "Blow the whistle!"

"Right on, brother!" Fitz said. And then he said, "And sister." Then he did a double-take and said, "Hey, wait a sec. You two twins or somethin'?"

That got us giggling, which got Fitz laughing. This trip of ours was beginning to look better and better.

"Now, take a look at this here," Fitz said. He meant this whole big panel of buttons and knobs and switches and lights that he was sitting right in front of. "See this mushroom thing?"

We told him we did. It wasn't no real mushroom, but it sure did look like a big metal one, and it grew straight up out of the middle of the control panel.

"Good," he said. "Now, take your hands on it, and when I say three, use some of them muscles you got and plunge it down. Got it?"

"Got it!"

"All right, now. One . . . two . . . and . . . THREE!"

We pushed hard, and that mushroom sank down beneath our push, and out came the long, loud toot we'd been hearing all our lives. The sound reverberated up from the floor and through our shoes and up our socks and even into the seats of our britches so that it tickled.

"Now let off and play her again."

We followed his directions, and once again our train howled, and once again our britches tingled.

"Good goin'," Fitz said. "Now give it just one more short tap for good measure."

We did that, too, and within no more than five seconds,

we crossed a deserted gravel road with a rusty STOP, LOOK & LISTEN sign posted right next to it.

"You two is pretty good musicians. That was an F-sharp you just played."

We looked at each other and smiled.

Then Fitz said, "Always my dream to blow the horn in a jazz band. But wasn't meant to be." He said that more to himself and his panel of knobs than to us. "Ain't no matter, though. Now, just sit back and enjoy the ride."

So we hopped back up on our throne and did what we were told and stared out the window at nothing but grass and sky and the two strips of iron cutting straight through it. We had lots of time to look and stare because we weren't even going that fast. A big number on a dial on Fitz's panel said 38 mph. And when you're in the middle of all that space, you can hardly tell you're moving anywhere. We reckoned it was a bit like being on a boat out in the middle of the ocean. We'd never seen so much nothing in all our lives.

"You mean this is what it looks like where we live?" we asked Fitz.

And Fitz said, "Yup. Pretty amazin', ain't it?"

While we took it all in, Fitz was constantly busy twisting knobs, flipping switches, and pushing buttons. But at some point he had a free moment and a free hand to offer us a container of smoked trout. "Caught and smoked it myself," he said.

Fish? Growing up in a place as dry as Wymore, the only fish we'd ever seen was in our schoolbooks.

"You just gotta know where to look for 'em," Fitz said. "Now, go ahead and use your fingers. The queen ain't comin' to dinner."

So even though we were still full of potluck, we thanked him and opened the container. And what we saw there was a real honest-to-goodness dead fish. If it hadn't been missing its tail and its head, you would've thought it could've swam away.

"Go on," Fitz said. "It ain't gonna bite ya."

And so, well, we started picking at the fish with our fingers just like he said we should. And you know what? It was real good! And so smoky that it dang near made our lungs cough.

"Just watch out for little bones," Fitz said, then blew the whistle, and we looked out the window, and sure enough, there was one of them posts with an X on it, just like he said there would be.

Time passed, and even though to us it didn't ever look like we were going past anything, Fitz kept pointing out landmarks to us left and right. "There's an old Indian burial mound right there."

We looked and squinted, but couldn't see no mound.

"See that little hump back off that way?" he asked a few minutes later.

"Hump?"

"Covered ammo during World War II."

Wasn't that in the last century?

"Look at that red-tail on that cottonwood over there!"

He kept going on like that, and that's how we got to see all the things that Fitz saw and we didn't.

And then there was all the towns we went through. Or rather what was left of them. Bunch of places we ain't never heard of. Hyannis. Mullen. Jewell. Ord. Yellville. Usually nothing left but a single shed or one lonesome brick building or a patch of blacktop stretching from nowhere to nothing or a tall grain elevator no longer in service. Our favorite was the town of Wunce.

"Check it out," Fitz said, and pointed. "Ain't nothing left but that there yellow DEAD END sign you see sticking up outta the bluestem."

"How come you know all this stuff?" we finally asked.

"Been working this stretch over ten years is how."

That was as long as we were alive! "Is that why your hat says 'MILES' for? For all the miles you done traveled?"

Then Fitz took off his hat and looked at it and said, "Yeah, guess it could mean that, too. Never thought of that."

But he didn't have a chance to tell us what it really meant because the control panel butted in and started to say something.

"Now en turr ing dark terr uh torr eee."

It was like a robot voice. "What was that?" we asked.

"That? Just the trackside scanner."

"The what?"

Fitz told us that his train automatically told him stuff, like if it had any defects or what the temperature was outside. And in this case, it was telling us that we were now entering dark territory.

So of course we had to ask, "What's dark territory?" Because it was as sunny as a song outside.

Fitz adjusted his cap and said, "It's kinda complicated. But basically it means I gotta talk to somebody directly on the radio to find out what I need to do instead of readin' my directions from off this chart here."

He flipped a switch and bent over and spoke into an

intercom thing built into the control panel. "CNABTB goin' dark," he said.

And about ten seconds later, a crackly voice came back out of the intercom and said, "All clear."

And that was it. Until about five minutes later, the robot said, "Now lee ving dark terr uh torr eee."

"Understand it this time?" Fitz asked us.

And we said, "'Now leaving dark territory'?"

"You got it! Couple of future engineers right here."

That made us feel good.

We traveled some more and looked out the windows at the dramatic and sensational[3] amount of empty space all around us. For a while we got to push the mushroom and blow the whistle about every mile or so, and soon thereafter we passed by a deserted road, and the whole time we ain't never once seen a single pickup. And the more we chugged along, now at only 26 mph, we started to get a bit drowsy from the sun and the rocking of the train and the slowness and the sameness of it all. If the cabin we were in had air conditioning, it sure wasn't working no good.

. . . .

3   It occurred to us out there that we'd kinda forgot about our good diction.

We yawned and asked, "What happens if you ever fall asleep out here?"

"I'll show you," Fitz said.

He didn't fall asleep or nothing, but he did stop fiddling with the control panel for the first time during our whole trip, and almost right away what sounded like a smoke detector went off and made us nearly jump clean through the roof. Fitz smiled and pushed down a different mushroom, and the screaming stopped.

"That's what happens," he said. "I stop workin' this here panel for fifteen seconds, that alarm goes off. Which'll wake you up no matter how loud you're snorin'. Way back a long time ago, you had to keep a foot pedal pushed down the whole time. Called a dead man's pedal. And if you let up on that thing, *bang*, the train stopped." And Fitz made the sound of brakes screeching. *Urrrrrrrrrchchch!*

"Speakin' of which," Fitz said, "I reckon it's about time we start slowin' her down."

"Aww!" we complained.

And Fitz said, "All good things must come to an end."

And we looked at him and said, "Except hot dogs."

And Fitz said, "Hot dogs?"

And we said, "Yeah, because they got two ends!"

Fitz laughed at that one so hard that he had to wipe his eyes afterward. "You two kids are all right."

Then he started playing his control panel with both hands, and we felt ourselves slowing down a bit and could even feel the weight of the train pushing up against the back of our seat. And before we knew it, Mr. Buzzard's yellow pickup came into view.

Fitz stopped the coal train right in front of Maggie's Crossing. We had imagined it was gonna be some great big flashing deal, but it was nothing more than another deserted dirt road with at most a jackrabbit running across it.

"Let's hustle down outta here before Maggie catches wind of us," Fitz said, and reached over and opened the door for us.

We took our school bag and climbed down, and when our feet touched the ground, the first thing we noticed was how still the earth was and not all vibrating like up on the train. Then we noticed how there was one sizzling hot wind blowing out there, with nothing around to stop it. No trees, no buildings, no nothing. Luckily we didn't see no lady in boots and a shotgun neither.

Fitz leaned out the window and said, "Been nice travelin' with you two kids!" He tipped his hat again that said MILES on it that we never learned how come, and we said

"Thanks, Fitz!" Then Fitz disappeared from the window, and we stood out next to Mr. Buzzard's truck and shaded our eyes and watched the train slowly pull away.

"Okay now, Stella. Jimmy. Time to crack the whip," said Mr. Buzzard.

But we weren't about to move before we found out how many cars our coal train had, and we'd already counted thirty-four, thirty-five, thirty-six . . .

"Okay, now, I ain't kiddin'. You don't wanna be late to Dixie's, do ya?"

Of course we didn't. But we was up to seventy-nine, eighty, eighty-one . . . and there still wasn't no end in sight.

"I'll go without you. I will, now. Just take that school bag of yours and head right on out . . . All right, then, here I goes. Openin' the door to my pickup . . ."

We heard his door moan worse than a haunted house, but we still didn't move none, since we were already up to hopper number 125 and counting.

"Okay, kids, listen, now. I'm climbin' right on in. And diggin' for the keys . . . Now, where'd I put them keys, any-how?"

We shouted when we busted the record at 133, and there was still even some coal train left to go. And it wasn't until we counted the caboose as number 145 that we yelled, "Okay, Mr. Buzzard, we're coming!" and scampered off to his pickup.

"Good thing, too," Mr. Buzzard said. "'Cause I was just about ready to pull off without ya. Now, get here in the cab. It's too hot out back."

That was fine with us, as much as we loved sitting out back in an old tire. But we were already overheated, and so we climbed up in through the driver's door because the other one didn't work anymore. Pops always said Mr. Buzzard's truck was held together by wire and a prayer.

Mr. Buzzard tried starting his pickup, but it wouldn't start. And it really did look like he was praying there, bent over the steering wheel like that with his eyes closed. Pops also said that Mr. Buzzard himself was about as handy as a back pocket on a shirt.

"It's hot in here," we said.

"You two kids just hold on to your saddle. Once we get goin', I'll turn this place into a meat locker."

Mr. Buzzard turned the ignition and pumped the gas pedal and whacked the dashboard and blew the horn and pumped the gas pedal and turned the ignition and whacked the dashboard and kept whispering something to himself about hail Mary. And long after we thought it was ever gonna be possible, his pickup started, and it was shakier than the train we were just on.

"See there? What'd I tell ya?" Mr. Buzzard said. "Now, watch this." He slid a knob on the AC over to the blue side, and almost immediately little pieces of ice started flying out of the vents. He wasn't kidding about that meat locker. And then we were off.

"We should be at Dixie's either in under thirty minutes or over sixty minutes, depending on if the truck breaks down."

That ended up being about the last thing we heard. Because once Mr. Buzzard's truck got going, it stopped being so shaky, and the air cooled down nice, and we got good and comfy on the beat-up old seat we were sitting on, and Mr. Buzzard turned on the radio and picked up a nice soft song about highways and heartaches. From all the excitement we'd been through that day, we were as beat as two eggs in a mixing bowl, and the next thing we knew, we were back in Wymore, and there was some drool on our chins, and our school box wasn't in our school bag anymore.[4]

· ·

4   We got on each other for falling asleep like that and didn't talk none at suppertime. And back in our room in the evening, we pretended we were more interested in keeping straight who came first, Millard Fillmore or Franklin Pierce. But we made up fast when the phone rang.

Chapter Twenty:

Sweet Voice

"SO, HOW WAS YOUR DAY?" Mom asked. We noticed she sounded awful chipper.

We said, "Day?" And we made faces at each other for not knowing what we should say. Until finally alls we said was, "Oh, not much."

But Mom pressed us like a pair of pants. "It was Train Day, though, wasn't it?"

"Train Day?" By then it was clear to us that we should've spent less time being mad at each other and more time preparing for Mom's call.

"You know, only your *favorite* day of the week?"

And we said, "Oh, *that* Train Day. Yeah . . . It was Train Day, Mom."

"Well, that's nice to hear," Mom said. "Thank you for telling me."

"You're welcome!"

"How many cars were there?"

That was an easy one. At least it should've been, since we set a new record. But on account of being nervous, we jumbled the numbers all up. "Four hundred fifty-one."

"Four hundred fifty-one?! Are you sure about that?" Mom asked.

"Five hundred forty-one!" we corrected ourselves incorrectly.

"Come, now," Mom said.

We were getting more cornered than a triangle. But then we saw our bulletin board full of presidents and thought we had a way out. "Mom?"

"Yes, dears?"

"Can we tell you something?"

"You know you can always tell me everything." Boy, was her voice sounding sweet.

"You promise not to get mad?"

"Well, that will depend, of course. But I'll try."

So we took a deep breath and said, "It's about our summer homework."

Mom laughed. "Is that all?"

"Well, it's just that we're not getting very far on it."

"I'm certain you'll both do just fine. You should go talk to Grandpa Chester. He's got the memory of an elephant. In fact, he helped your Pops and me when we had to take that test."

We told Mom we'd be sure and talk to Grandpa Chester

the very next day. So long as he'd talk to us, that is.[1] And for the rest of our conversation, we did our best to talk about the presidents and were never gladder about that summer homework than just then.

It seemed like Mom was happy to talk about presidents too. She even told us some funny stories about them, like how George Washington had his horse's teeth brushed every day, and how Thomas Jefferson once got sent a thousand-pound hunk of cheese. She even knew that Millard Fillmore installed the first bathtub at the White House.

Our phone call swam along like a fish, and before we knew it, it was time to hang up. That was a relief, because we didn't enjoy fibbing to Mom like that for so long.

Mom must've been waiting for that very moment. "Oh, before I go, what was the name of the engineer again?"

We said, "You mean Fitz?" And then we said, "Oops!" and covered our mouths like a hole in our britches.

But in the sweetest voice we ever heard her speak, Mom just said, "I'm glad you had such a good time."

· ·

1   Because he didn't much like being interrupted when he was listening to a ball game.

Chapter Twenty-One:

Operation
Beautification

YOU NEVER WOULD'VE believed your own eyes had they seen the bustle and enterprise that swept through Wymore like a dust storm the following day. Truth be told, we had a hard time believing our eyes ourselves.

We were up in Old Tom Wood, flicking ants off our bare knees and reciting the presidents, and Jimmy was sucking on a nickel because that was Secret Trick #3 on how to get a loose tooth to fall out. And on account of that that's where we were, we missed it when the phone rang at Mabel's. It was Pops calling with good news. And the good news was that he liked the looks of the dingsbums all right and that he'd be on his way to Wymore no later than last week, by which he meant as soon as possible.

That was when we heard our names being hollered like the roof was on fire. We jumped right off Old Tom Wood like a pair of frogs. And that was how Jimmy finally got that loose tooth out[1] because upon landing he banged it on his knee just like how he got it loose in the first place.

· ·

1   As well as swallowing a nickel.

Jimmy stuck it deep in his pocket, and we ran off to Mabel's faster than a lit fuse.

We didn't even make it in the screen door before we were met by a stream of grandmas and grandpas on their way out. "What's going on?" we asked.

For an answer what we got was a paper place mat. We didn't know what to make of it until Grandma Ida appeared at the door with her dishrag on her shoulder and told us to turn it over.[2] When we did, we saw the words "Operation Beautification" wrote up at the top and underneath it a list of things to do as long as a garden hose. That was something we wanted to be a part of, so we asked, "How can we help out?"

Grandma Ida smiled and mussed up our hair some and cracked her gum loud as a bat hitting a ball and said, "Help out? We put you in charge!"

And the next thing we knew, she produced a clipboard, and we clipped the place mat to it. We thought it would've been nice to have a whistle hanging around our necks like a coach, but unfortunately we didn't have one.

Grandma Ida told us it was our job to make sure Operation Beautification was running smooth and all our

. . . .

2 The place mat, that is, not her dishrag.

grandparents were doing their jobs right. We said we could do that. But before we went to make our rounds, Jimmy smiled real big for her and showed her the lost tooth.

"Make sure you tuck it under your pillow tonight," she said. Then she dug around in her apron pocket and pulled out a quarter for each of us.

"Thanks, Grandma Ida!" we said. And off we ran.

We spent the next few hours overseeing the beautification and renovation of the Wymore town square. We saw to it that our grandmas had a fresh supply of soapy water and piles of rags to wipe off the clunkers clean as spit, right down to the side-view mirrors and whatever fenders still remained. We made a point of showing them Jimmy's tooth and collected three dimes and two nickels each. We helped our grandpas pump air into the flat tires until each one looked as big as a belly. Then Jimmy opened wide, and we took in two quarters and eight pennies.

From there we walked over to Grandma Elsie, who was busy pulling weeds out of the cracks in the sidewalk. She flashed us a green thumb, and Jimmy flashed her a smile that was good for four nickels.

Back in the middle of the square, Grandma Pearl prospected another rusty nail out of the ground. That gave us an idea. We told her them nails of hers might look real good in a little display case. We told her she could call it "Ancient Artifacts from Wymore." You should've saw the way her face brightened up like stars in a nighttime sky. Then Jimmy smiled, and we collected over a whole dollar just from her alone.

We wanted to visit Grandpa Bert next, but him and his broom was circulating the dust better than a fan. So we kept our distance and just called out to him to keep up the good work, even though that meant giving up a nickel or a dime. But we did go over to the old appliance store and help Grandpa Jarvis spruce up his storefront window. We put price tags on the rusty stove and the icebox that was missing a door. And after we were done, Grandpa Jarvis went behind the counter and got his cigar box and pulled out a quarter for each of us. When we smiled and he spotted Jimmy's missing tooth, he added another nickel.

From there it was back across the street to where four of our grandpas were sitting side by side on a bench like birds on a telephone wire. They were scrubbing rust from the missing letters to the hotel sign, each of them using a different method. The *S* grandpa was using baking soda, and the *T* grandpa was employing vinegar, and the *L* grandpa was utilizing aluminum foil dipped in water, and the *E* grandpa was applying lemon juice and salt. Orange dust fell to their feet pretty as snow. They were arguing over whose method was working best, and the only way we could get them to stop was by showing them Jimmy's tooth. None of them wanted to look stingy, so we walked away with a handful of coins.

Over at the beauty parlor, Grandma Francine was trying out different wigs on the bald lady mannequin in the window. She had it narrowed down to one wig called "Halo Curly," one named "Spiked Expression," and one wig referred to as "Bed Head." We liked that one best because that was how our hair looked most of the time. But even though we were the ones who were supposed to be in charge, Grandma Francine eventually picked "Halo Curly" and pulled it onto the dummy's head like a winter cap. Jimmy smiled, and she gave us both a quarter.

A few doors down, Grandpa Virgil was out giving the stripes on the barber pole a fresh coat of paint while Grandpa Homer held the three different cans of color for him.

"You ain't staying in the lines, Grandpa Virgil," we said.

And Grandpa Homer said, "I keep telling him the same thing!"

That made us laugh, considering how Grandpa Homer ain't seen lines or nothing else for years now.

But Grandpa Virgil said, "Once this pole is spinning again, you won't know the difference."

"You think you can get it to work again?" we asked.

"If you run over to Ickler's and find me an oil squirter, I will."

So you see, being in charge ain't nothing to snuff at because we were off once more at a full run. And while we were at the hardware store, we got another idea. We took an empty jar from a shelf and twisted off the lid and blew out the dust inside of it and sneezed. Then we poured all our coins into it and twisted the lid back on. After making our delivery to Grandpa Virgil, we went around to the back kitchen door at the café, where we heard Grandma Mabel's knife thwacking on the butcher block.

We walked in and saw her working at the prep table before she saw us. And we just reached out with our jar and said, "Here, Grandma Mabel."

And Grandma Mabel asked, "What'cha got there?"

And we said, "Tooth Fairy money. So you don't have to close down."

If we had known she was gonna go and turn on the waterworks like that again, we might've kept the money for ourselves and sent away for a pair of x-ray glasses we saw advertised in the back of an old magazine. But it was too late.

Once Grandma Mabel got her face mopped up with the corner of her apron, she went to her big white fridge and brought us each back a chocolate pudding she called a dusty miller.[3] And we smiled because it had been a real long time since we'd had one of them.

So we whispered something to each other and then took the jar of coins back off the table, and Jimmy dug around in his pocket and pulled out his tooth and added it to the jar. "You can keep whatever the Tooth Fairy gives you for it," we said.

Then we left fast as we could before Grandma Mabel got teary on us again.

. . . .

3 That's because there was a nice layer of cocoa powder resting on top just waiting for you to sweep up with your spoon.

Chapter Twenty-Two:

Our Palace

WE TOOK OUR DUSTY MILLERS and sat out on the bench right next to Grandpa Chester. Desserts ain't never taken us long to eat, and soon we were done and swinging our legs some, since our feet didn't touch the ground. Eventually we got up the nerve and asked Grandpa Chester, "Who's winning?"

Usually he'd just say a team name, maybe the score. If you were real lucky and happened to ask him during a commercial break, he might tell you what inning it was. So our surprise couldn't have been bigger when Grandpa Chester pulled the radio from his ear and clicked it off with his thumb and said, "It don't matter. Ain't nuthin' but a game."

"We always thought you liked baseball, Grandpa Chester," we said. *Breathed* baseball would've been more like it.

"I do," he said. "But I ain't so interested in who wins and who loses. Be it the Turkeys, the Roadrunners, or the Hyenas."

"Them ain't no baseball teams."

"Ain't they, now? Well, then, what are some?"

So we named him several, and then a couple more. Then when he griped at us for stopping halfway, we came up with three more on top of that.

Grandpa Chester nodded his head and said, "You'll get there."

And we asked, "Get where?"

But he didn't tell us where. Instead he said, "The real reason I listen to baseball is to stay fit."

And we laughed because we thought he was pulling our drumsticks. How do you stay fit sitting on a bench all day with a transistor radio at your ear?

We were about to say as much, but Grandpa Chester got his say in first. "Honus Wagner. Otherwise knowed as the Flying Dutchman. 1900. 580 plate appearances, 201 hits, 45 doubles, 22 triples, 4 homers. Exactly 100 runs batted in. 38 stolen bases, 41 walks. Striked out a mere 17 times. Batting average of .381." And right when we thought he was finished, he added, "Oh, yeah, and he got hit by a pitch 8 times. Though I have to admit I couldn't tell you where exactly."

That's when we started to understand what he meant by fit. "Can you do that with any other players?"

"Darn near each and every one of 'em. And every season too. But only back to the year 1900, as I was just workin' on when you sat down with your puddin'. Chocolate, I do believe it was."

Now we knew why Mom said we should come and have a talk with him about our homework. "You think you can help us remember the presidents like that?"

"Ain't a pupil that growed up in Wymore that I haven't. Includin' your Mom and Pops. She tell you that?"

"She did."

"And they both got an A if I'm remembering right."

That sounded good to us. "Well, what do we gotta do to get an A?"

"Ain't much to it," Grandpa Chester said. "Once you choose your palace."

And we said, "Huh?" Living in Wymore, we ain't never seen a single palace.

Grandpa Chester said it was as easy as falling off a log. He explained to us his trick in three little steps. "First you gotta pick a place you know good as your back pocket. That's what's called your palace. Then once you got that, alls you gotta do is picture all the different details about it. You followin'?"

We weren't really. And so we asked, "What's your palace?"

And Grandpa Chester said, "We're sittin' right across from it."

We looked across the street, past Grandma Winnie wiping off a clunker and over Grandma Elsie, who was bent down pulling weeds, and there was the old drugstore. Its sign was missing lots of letters, too, and now it just spelled out RU ST.

"That's your palace?"

"That it is. Stood in there behind the counter for darn near forty years, and there ain't no nook, cranny, or apothecary jar in there that I ain't on a first-name basis with."

"Apotha-canary what?" we asked.

"That's them dusty jars up on the shelves with them funny words on 'em. Alum, Junip., Sod. Bromide, Sulph. Forty-two of 'em in all, and I still know each and every one. Left to right and right to left. Which is what I'm sayin'. Find a place you know inside out and outside in. And that, kids, will be your palace."

Now we were starting to get it. We put our heads together, and it didn't take us long. "Can we pick Mabel's?"

"I'd say there ain't no better choice to be choosed," Grandpa Chester answered.

"But what do we do with it?"

"Just think about some of the things that are in there."

Well, that wasn't hard. We named stuff like how the screen door's always stuck, and how our booth's by the window, and them greasy bottles of ketchup and mustard on the table. We mentioned that jar of relish we won't touch, the tricycle stain and the boat stain up on the ceiling, and the TV up in the corner that's always going on and on about the weather. Then there was the fan rotating back and forth all summer long on the lunch counter, the library booth with its pile of old books, and them swinging doors leading back to Grandma Mabel in the kitchen.

We could've kept going, but where did all the presidents come in at?

"That's step three," Grandpa Chester said. "Now what you do is, you tell yourself a story. Because stories is how you remember things. Just ask Grandpa Homer and Grandpa Virgil. And in that story, you make each president have somethin' to do with each of them things you've just been tellin' me about: the screen door, the stains, the relish."

"You mean like George Washington opened the screen door?"

"That's the general idea. But the funnier you make it, the easier you're gonna remember."

We thought for a moment and asked, "George Washington pulled and tugged, but couldn't open the screen door?"

Grandpa Chester smacked his hands together. "Much better!"

"And John Adams looked up at the tricycle stain?"

"Why not say that John Adams *rode* the tricycle stain?"

"And Thomas Jefferson sailed on the boat stain?"

"Bingo! People's always saying he was the smart one of the bunch."

That's when we started having fun with it. We sat James Madison down in our booth and had him order a groundhog,[1] and James Monroe served him one slathered with yucky relish. John Quincy Adams wasn't hungry and went to the library to read *Lectures on the True, the Beautiful, and the Good,* while Andrew Jackson just sat there throwing a hissy fit about the weather report. The weatherman on the TV was Martin Van Buren, and he was saying, "Looks like it's gonna be another scorcher," and that was why William Henry Harrison was up at the lunch counter hogging

. . . .

1   Just a hot dog.

the fan. And before we knew it, we were already up to nine presidents!

"Who taught you this trick, Grandpa Chester?" we asked.

And he said, "Read about it in some book long time back. Some kinda encyclopedia or somethin'. Funny, but can't seem to remember the title just now."

We looked at each other and knew what we were thinking.[2]

"Well, I guess I'll be gettin' back to my ball game," Grandpa Chester said with a wink, and stuck his transistor radio up against his ear. And we were certain we heard bat strike ball and the crowd roar.

. . . .

2   Did Grandpa Chester mean *The Handy Cyclopedia of Things Worth Knowing*? We later found out he did. Page 479.

Chapter Twenty-Three:
A Light Flickers

WE GRABBED OUR CLIPBOARD and made another round through town. Several clunkers were reflecting the sunlight for the first time in years, and near half the tires were still holding air. Grandma Elsie had a garbage pail full of weeds, and even though Grandpa Bert was brown with dust, the sidewalks looked as clean as a dish. A poster in the appliance store window read SUMMER SALE! The barbershop pole was turning sometimes, to the tune of an awful squeak, and up on the hotel roof we saw our grandpas nailing up the sign. The letters looked good now. The only problem was a couple of them were in the wrong place. We yelled, but our grandpas must've had their hearing aids unplugged. And that's how our hotel came to be called the Slantey.

Being beautificationists kept us busy till the shadows grew long. But in between things, we still had the chance to work on our presidents some. Millard Fillmore became the bubble dancer[1] with a sink full of pots and pans to

1 Which means he was the dishwasher.

waltz with, and Franklin Pierce was at the prep table pluck-ing a chicken.[2] And by dot nine o'clock that night when Mom called, we were already down to Rutherford B. Hayes and James A. Garfield, two guys we never could've remem-bered otherwise. Now Rutherford was studying a book called *How to Win at Checkers* while Garfield kept showing off the new anchor tattoo he had on his left bicep.

We ran our story by Mom, and she said, "Sounds like you had a good talk with Grandpa Chester."

And we asked her, "He ever tell you about the Flying Dutchman?"

She said, "Honus Wagner? Sure. He got hit by a pitch once in the 1917 season. But I couldn't tell you where ex-actly."

After we got off the phone with Mom, we still weren't in the mood for sleeping, even though we were yawning like we were getting paid for it. So we went over to our win-dow and breathed in deep against the screen and worked on our story a little more.[3]

. . . .

2   For now, we leapfrogged over presidents ten through twelve because their names aren't near as funny.

3   James K. Polk now got whacked on the biscuit by the swinging kitchen doors, and James Buchanan was chasing a fly down with a fly swat.

"Hey, look at that, Jimmy James."

"What?"

"Streetlight's flickerin'."[4]

"Sure is. We better get it fixed."

"Otherwise them June bugs won't have no place to congregate at."

"Shoot, they can fly off to McFall. They got more than enough lights up there."

"That's true."

"But I'll tell you one thing, Stella."

"What's that, Jimmy James?"

"We ain't goin' with 'em."

. . . .

4   And you'll remember, it's the only one that still worked.

Chapter Twenty-Four

What a Difference a Day Makes

M

EARLY NEXT MORNING a deep and long horn blast rattled the windows. And although the sun hadn't as yet been able to pry our eyelids open, that horn sure did. We knew right away that it was Pops's horn, and that got us moving faster than a drumroll.

We threw back our sheets and ran to the window just in time to see his big rig pull into the square and make that big sigh noise it always did when it came to a full stop. Then Pops's door opened, and we watched him climb down all stiff and sore at the back and then stand in the dusty square and stretch his arms out and scratch his beard and spit out a seed of some kind into the dirt. We're pretty sure Pops is the only trucker who ever wore a beret.

The next big surprise was that the other door opened, and there was Mom. She looked kinda dizzy standing way up there, so Pops went around to help her out and lifted her down with one arm and placed her gently as a feather on the ground. Then he reached back up into the cab and pulled out a little box with a bunch of stickers stuck all over it, and we knew right then and there that it was our school box.

We didn't bother none with our hair, and we didn't care about our faces, and we didn't give a hoot about what kinda crud might be stuck behind our ears. We just dashed clean out of our room still in our PJs and up the hall and down the stairs and through the lobby and out the door of the hotel[1] and into the sun and across the square and right into Mom's and Pops's waiting arms. Everybody smothered everybody else in hugs so much until none of us could breathe anymore and we had to come up for air.

The first thing we said was, "Show us the dingsbums!"

Pops said, "Dingsbums? What in the heck's a dingsbums?" He jiggled our school box up above his head just to make us squirm some.

But that was all right because we already knew what it looked like. Besides, we had lots to show them. And as we made our way over to Mabel's, we kept pointing at all the changes that had taken place in town under our supervision, and Mom and Pops couldn't stop marveling at how nice the square looked.

Mom said, "What a difference a day makes . . ."

. . . .

1 Whatever it was called now.

Actually she sung it, and her voice sparkled like honey.

And we said, "Hey, that's one of them songs Grandpa Homer and Grandpa Virgil sings!"

Then Pops picked up the tune and sung the next line. And we shouted, "Aww, Pops!" and covered our ears.

Pops cleared his throat and said, "Guess my singing days is over."

And Mom said, "I hadn't realized they ever started!"

Once we got to Mabel's, Pops grabbed the screen door and jerked hard on it until it opened and said, "On tray voo!"[2] It sure was great to be all together again.

It must've still been early because there wasn't no one else in the diner, and Grandma Ida was still busy laying place mats. Mom and Pops went to thank her kindly for looking after us all week, and we saved their spots for them at our booth and couldn't sit close enough to make up for all the lost time.

Grandma Ida followed right up with two cups of joe for Mom and Pops and a large glass of moo juice[3] for each of us. "What kinda birdseed can I get y'all this morning?" she asked.

. . . .

2 More of Pops's French we can't spell. This one means "Enter!"
3 You can probably figure out on your own what that is.

Mom ordered an Adam and Eve on a raft,[4] and Pops went for a bowl of red, heavy on the breath[5] because that's just the type of thing he likes eating in the morning. We asked for checkerboards with extra axle grease.[6]

Then Pops said, "Ain't you two turkeys gonna have a look?"

He was talking about our school box, which was sitting right in the middle of the table. We reached over and opened it up. There was our dingsbums—along with about ten other dingsbumses mixed in with it. We didn't know what that was supposed to mean.

Pops said, "Spark plugs! Just like I thought. So I picked up a few more of 'em on my way into town. I reckon one of 'em's gonna get that hippomobile up and runnin'."

"You mean you can just buy a dingsbums nowadays?"

"If you got a couple bucks in your pocket you can," Pops said.

"Does that mean that all this time the hippomobile could've been working, and that alls it needed was a dumb old spark plug?"[7] we asked.

. . . .

4 That's eggs on toast.
5 That's chili con carne with extra onions.
6 And that's butter.
7 We'll admit that we don't know what dumb old spark plugs are for.

"I dunno," Pops said. "But that's what I'm doing here to find out."

That was when Grandma Ida arrived with the food. "Clear the runway!" she called out before putting our plates down.

Pops rubbed his hands and said, "Bone appatee!" Which was more French for "Enjoy your meal."

And we did, too, all of us working our elbows and filling our shirts like we were Family Grubstruck. Mom only interrupted our chewing once or twice to have Jimmy show her that hole in his mouth again. Otherwise no one spoke anything until Pops put his spoon down in his empty bowl and patted his stomach twice and said, "So, let's go!"

But before we could even say "Yeah!" Mom said, "Smitty, wipe your mouth."[8]

Pops said, "On the road it's a sign of respect to leave a little somethin' clingin' to your beard when you eat."

Mom just said, "Wipe it!" And he did. But she wasn't finished, neither. Because to us she said, "Go get your helmets!"

And we said, "Aww, Mom!"

. . . .

8   Smitty is what she calls him sometimes when he is doing something she doesn't like.

And Pops said, "Aww, Mom!"

But Mom just said, "Helmets! And while you're there, put some clothes on!"

We knew there wasn't gonna be no discussing the matter, so we ran back to the hotel and did as we were told. By the time we returned to Mabel's, Pops was outside with a can of gas and having a closer look at that screen door.

"Where's Mom?" we asked.

Pops just said, "She needs another cup of joe. Too much dancin' last night. But don't tell her I said that." And he winked.

So it was just the three of us, and Pops couldn't get over how good the square looked.

"And we were in charge, too," we said.

Pops looked at the items on sale at the appliance store, and the lady in the beauty parlor window, and the sign on top of the hotel that read SLANTEY, and he said, "I can tell."

That made us feel real good.

No one else was out and about yet, and as we made our way to Hill Street, we didn't even come across Grandpa Milton walking his old mail route. We tried tugging on Pops to get him to go faster, but he either wouldn't or couldn't, and there wasn't a thing we could do about it.

When we finally got to the old factory building and saw the battered door, we slapped ourselves square on our foreheads. We forgot all about the key.

But Pops said, "Key? Who needs a key? C'mon!"

So we shrugged our shoulders and followed him around through the weeds and out to the back of the building, where there was a big barn-door kind of a door.

Pops tried prying open the latch. "This is how we snuck in here back when we was kids," he said. "Thing's all warped now, though. You're gonna have to loan me some of your iron."

So we all grabbed that latch and on the count of twa,[9] we gave it all we had and then some. What happened next was the latch busted clean off. That made the barn door start to wobble. Then it swung wide open and came right off its hinges and teetered just long enough for us to jump out of the way. Then it fell toward the grass with one big *whoosh!* and hit the ground with one big *whump!*

We all stood there looking at it a second, and then Pops scratched his head and said, "Guess I know what I'll be doing tomorrow." By which he meant fixing it back together.

· ·

9 That's "three" in French.

Then we walked into the building, and there stood the hippomobile. We could tell that the sight of it nearly blew Pops's beret clean off. He said, "Dang!" and that was it. It was a long time later before he said, "I bet I ain't been in here in over thirty years." The whole time he was walking around real slow and running his hand over the hippomobile and enjoying the moment like it was a plate of meat and gravy. And then he said, "You believe that? We used to sit up on this thing for hours playing stagecoach." But it wasn't even like he was talking to us or even knew we were still there.

After a while we couldn't take it anymore and said, "Pops. Hey, Pops!"

He snapped out of it like a rubber band. "What's up?"

"You all right?"

"Yeah, my back's just fine."

"We didn't mean your back."

But Pops just said, "Gimme that school box of yours."

We gave it to him, and he went over to the hippomobile and found his footing in one of the wheel spokes and started climbing right up. The hippomobile protested with more groans than school kids on test day, but it didn't fall apart like we were fearing it was gonna.

Once Pops was up on top, he said, "Hot diggity! Feel like a kid again."

"Can we climb up too?"

"I sure hope so."

It didn't take us much more than a hop, skip, and a jump to get up there, but even so, Pops was already prying open the lid to the wood box up by the steering wheel by the time we arrived. When he lifted it off, we bent over to look in and were surprised to see all kinds of gears and pulleys in there.

We looked at each other and whispered, "That must be the engine."

Meanwhile Pops was busy rubbing his beard and looking hard at those gears and pulleys. "That Gottfried was smart as a sore thumb," he said.

"He was?"

Pops didn't bother with answering us. He was making that clicking sound with his tongue that meant he was thinking. Plus he was busy poking his finger around all the parts in the engine box. Every once in a while he said things like "Well, I'll be!" and "No kiddin'!" And it wasn't a minute too soon for us when he finally said, "Now where'd that school box take off to?"

"Here it is, Pops!" We handed it to him and even opened the lid for him. "Which one you think you're gonna use?"

Pops just said, "I'll find out as soon as I know."

That meant not to bug him about it. So we sat there on the front bench quiet as a puddle and watched him try one dingsbums after another until we lost track of how many he done tried. Eventually he pulled a wrench out of one of his pockets and went to work with that some. Then he went back to trying to find the right dingsbums. The whole time our fingers were crossed so hard, they nearly snapped like twigs.

Then sudden as a thunderclap, Pops said, "You gotta be kiddin'!"

And we said, "What, Pops?"

And Pops said, "That old dingsbums you found fits after all. Had the dang thing in backwards and upside down to boot." And then he added, "But don't you go tellin' no one."

And we said, "It's between us and the fence post."

Then Pops said, "Well, let's get rollin'!"

"You mean we're gonna start it up?" we asked.

And Pops said, "You didn't think we was gonna stand around singin' to it, did ya?"

We just covered our ears.

Chapter Twenty-Five:

Blue-Plate Special

POPS TOLD US TO START the engine. We looked up and down the steering wheel for a keyhole,[1] and since we didn't find one, we inspected the engine box. We didn't have any luck there, either, so we stood up and turned around to inspect the seat we were sitting on. The whole time Pops kept going, "Warmer, warmer . . ." and then, "Cold. Very cold. Bitter cold," and you could tell he was enjoying himself. But at some point he had us so cold, our teeth were rattling, and we clean gave up.

Pops got a big laugh outta the whole deal. "What you're lookin' for is right there in front of your beaks," he said, and pointed to a black curved metal bar sticking out of the right side of the engine box.

"That ain't no key, Pops."

And Pops said, "You're right. It's a crank."

And we said, "Huh?"

. . . .

1 It didn't occur to us that we didn't have a key for it.

Pops explained to us that back then you didn't start a pickup with a key—you had to crank it started.

And we said, "You mean like a jack-in-the-box?"

"Yup. But just don't expect no weasel to go poppin' out of the engine. Now, go ahead and wind her up."

The crank was big enough for all four of our hands, and we worked together hard as a walnut, but it wouldn't budge none.

Pops shook his head and asked, "Am I gonna have to go get the spinach or somethin'?"

"No spinach!" And with the help of some elbow grease, we finally got the crank cranking.

"There you go!" Pops shouted.

We kept that crank moving around in circles like a dog after its tail, but the hippomobile didn't seem to care none. It just sat there all peaceful and quiet, and we finally had to give up and take a breather.

"You two ain't plannin' on walkin' back, is you?"

We'd show Pops what we were planning and not planning to do! This time we spit on our hands and rubbed it in real good and got that crank whizzing like an airplane propeller.

And Pops said, "Atta way!"

But the hippomobile still sat there lazy as a Sunday afternoon, and there wasn't anything left for us to do but to give up. Even Pops said, "Booger," and took off his beret and scratched his head.

"Maybe we should put some gas in it," we said.

"Gas." Pops repeated the word like he was spitting out a piece of gristle. "It ain't called gas—it's called *fuel*."

"Well, maybe we should put some fuel in it. You brought the can and all."

"Don't you think I done thought of that?"

We could tell that was one of them questions we wasn't supposed to answer, probably because he forgot all about it.

Pops let a little time go by and then said, "Where is that gas can, anyhow?"

"You mean the fuel can?"

"Just gimme the can."

We did so and watched him pour like a mad scientist in a laboratory. We leaned back and had our faces covered just in case a cloud of something rose up out of the tank. But that ain't what happened. Instead came this sputtering and coughing and vibrating from underneath that reminded us of a busted ride at the county fair.

Pops yelled out, "Crank it, you turkeys!"

And we did. And the more we did, the more the hippomobile shuddered and shimmied and coughed like it needed a good slap on the back. Then the engine sorta went *vroom!* Pops told us to hold off, and we stopped cranking. And sure as a cow tail swats flies, the hippomobile kept on vibrating all on its very own.

Pops said, "Good goin', you turkeys!"

But we didn't have time for celebrating because something else started to happen. "What's going on?" we asked.

Pops just laughed. "You better put on them helmets of yours. 'Cause we're rollin'!"

And indeed we were! Not too fast maybe, and you probably could've walked backwards on one sore foot faster than we were traveling, but there was no doubting the fact that we really were on our way right out the factory door. So we put on our helmets and fastened the straps secure under our chins and couldn't help but feel like we were out on the speedway.

Pops told us to scoot it and grabbed the wheel. "Let's just hope them axles hold," he said. Once we left the building, he needed to steer the hippomobile around back the other direction toward town. "Help me out some and lean hard to the left."

We leaned like saplings in a windstorm, and Pops

worked like crazy to get the steering wheel to turn, and the hippomobile began creaking louder than attic steps. But nothing busted, and soon us and the hippomobile were turned around the right way and on Hill Street and slowly heading back into town.

"This ol' thing handles pretty good!" Pops said.

We were about to agree, but just then the hippomobile stopped in its tracks and might've bucked us clean off if we'd been going any faster. "Hey!" we yelled.

Pops's hand came down with a loud smack on the engine box. And believe it or not, that got the hippomobile running again, all right. But it started running backwards.

"Hey, Pops, we're going the wrong way!"

Pops gave us that one look that said, "Thanks for telling me." He started looking all over for some kinda knob or switch to change directions.

He looked kinda funny, but we weren't about to say "Cold, colder!" or nothing like that. Instead we just took a chance and gave the engine box another smack, but this time on the other side. And lo and behold, that did the trick! The hippomobile stopped, rumbled in place for a moment like an upset stomach, and then set back off in the direction we were wanting to go.

"Looks like I'm gonna have to work out a few kinks in

this thing," Pops said. Then he moved over and let us take the wheel. "Easy does it."

And there we were, riding for real on top of the hippomobile just like Gottfried Schuh! It was almost like a Sunday drive. The only thing missing was a radio and a window to hang your arm out of. We sure couldn't wait to show Mom.

We began veering a bit rightward, and Pops said, "Hold her steady, now."

And so we leaned left and gave the steering wheel a nice gentle twist. It twisted just fine. In fact, it twisted clean off.

"Pops! Look!"

And Pops said, "Holy potato! Gimme that thing quick!"

We handed it to him and held on tight as the hippomobile ran off the road and began mowing down weeds. Pops worked double time to get the steering wheel to fit back in, and we didn't bother him none except for yelling out, "Tree!" and then, "TREE!" and then finally, *"TREE!"*

But lucky for us and the hippomobile, Pops was able to snap the wheel back in just in the nick of time and avoid the tree trunk. We did run through some branches, though, and were forced to eat a few leaves. And Pops darn near got his beret snatched off.

"Mon dew!" Pops called out in some French we didn't get. "That was closer than my shadow!"

He stayed in the driver's seat and got us back on the blacktop, and for a while we were happy to be the copilots. But once we turned off Hill Street without anything unordinary happening, Pops said we should have the honors of driving the home stretch.

We were smiling so much, our cheeks hurt. This time we made sure to keep the hippomobile right in the middle of the road. When we went by our oak tree, we waved and yelled, "Thanks, Old Tom Wood!" If it hadn't been for Old Tom Wood, who knows if we would've found Gottfried Schuh's old letter to begin with.

Then we had just one more block to go. We couldn't wait to see the looks on everybody's faces as we drove into town. Except it turned out that we were the ones in for the big surprise. Just before we entered the square, we saw a big banner stretched across the street from the top of one building to the top of another. It was made out of old sheets, and the words painted on it read

WELCOME TO WYMORE
HOME OF THE HIPPOMOBILE

Pops said, "Didn't turn out too bad, did it?"

We looked up at him and said, "You mean you knew about it?"

But we didn't hear his answer because then we saw something else, and our jaws dropped down to our knees. It was Mom, and she was up on the one roof holding the banner steady. She was wearing a helmet, but it was her all right, and that might've been the first time she'd ever been up on a roof in all her life.[2] And yet there she was, waving and smiling proud. And up on the other roof was Grandma Ida. She pulled a camera out of her apron pocket and started taking snapshots.[3] And since the hippomobile was going so slow, we even had enough time to make several silly faces.

Then we crossed under the banner, and the whole dusty town square came into full view. All our grandpas and grandmas were lining the street in their best bib overalls and button-down blouses and waving the flags that otherwise came out only for Train Day. We waved back to everybody, and it was almost like being in a real parade, except that parades usually don't crash.

. . . .

2   It was certainly the first time she'd been up on a roof in all *our* lives.
3   One of the pictures she took landed us on the front page of the *McFall Dispatch*.

Pops said, "Now we've just gotta figure out how to stop this contraption."

We started looking around down at our feet for some kinda brake, but it didn't seem like Gottfried Schuh had gotten around to putting one in.

Pops said, "You gotta be kiddin' me!"

We squeezed the horn, but it just blew out a cloud of dust. So we started working our lungs. "Outta the way!" we yelled. We waved our arms like windmills to make sure we had everyone's attention. And in all that commotion, we didn't realize that we were holding the steering wheel clean up in the air.

Apparently our grandmas and grandpas did, though. As we started edging off the street and right toward Mabel's, they parted faster than the sea. Some ran for cover back into the café, and others hid behind a lamp pole, and a few climbed up on the bench Grandpa Chester always sat on.

Meanwhile we kept right on inching toward disaster and stomping with our feet for a brake that wasn't there while Pops fiddled with the steering wheel. Unfortunately, one of our stomps must've caught Pops's toes because he let out quite an "Ow!" and dropped the steering wheel. Alls we could do was watch it roll clean off the hippomobile, land on the ground, and keep right on rolling.

So now all three of us started smacking the engine box in the hopes of getting it to stop or even go backwards again. But in the end what saved us from running through Mabel's screen door was nothing more than the plain old curb. The hippomobile hit it square on but didn't have enough oomph to get up over it, so we came to a stop.

For a moment there, no one dared to move a muscle. But then smoke started rising up out of the engine box higher than a woodpecker's hole, and the front wheel fell off, and that was when we figured it was time to bail.

Mom was down in the crowd by then, and we heard her shout, "No jumping!" But it was too late because we were already standing back up and dusting the dust off our knees.

It took Pops a little longer to get down, but once he did and got a kink out of his back, he came over and stood with us in front of Mabel's and watched and listened to the hippomobile shake, shudder, cough, and blow more smoke than a chimney. We didn't have to wait long before a back wheel gave out. Then the other back wheel gave out, and the whole shebang fell flat to the ground and turned silent as a stone. And for a stretch, alls you could hear was the ringing in your ears.

No one said nothing. Mom pulled us closer in to her. Some people covered their mouths with their hands. Some of our grandmas made the sign of the cross, and our grandpas removed their hats. There our future was, lying flattened out as a toad on the road. It wasn't hard to figure out that this wasn't a good development. And just when we thought nothing couldn't get no worse, the banner came loose and went flapping down to the ground like a ghost gone haywire. And still no one ain't said nothing.

Then Pops went over to the hippomobile and kneeled down best he could and examined one of them wheels and took a close look at an axle and said, "Looks like I know what else I'll be doin' tomorrow."

We almost didn't dare ask. But we did, just not too loud. "You mean you think you can fix it?"

Pops turned around and looked at us. "You askin' an old grease monkey that?"

That's when the whole town of Wymore, all fifty-one of us, broke out in a cheer louder than a stampede. Everybody walked up and inspected the hippomobile and ran their hands over it like a long-lost pet. Many grandmas and grandpas shook their heads in silent wonder, several debated how long it'd been since they'd last saw it, and quite a few wiped their eyes.

At some point Pops said, "Yeah, you gotta hand it to that ol' Gottfried. He built himself one robust and rugged contraption."

We looked at each other and said, "Pops, how did you know that phrase?"

Pops said, "Saw it in some old book I used to look at back when I was a little kid. It's where I learned my French at, too." Then he grinned and said, "Now, where's that Mabel at?"

Everybody called for Grandma Mabel, and she finally stepped out of the crowd in her white apron and chef hat.

"I hear you're open for business," said Pops.

We could tell that Grandma Mabel didn't know what to say at first. She looked all around at everybody else. When we all nodded our heads, she finally turned back to Pops and said, "I reckon I am."

And Pops said, "Then gimme a blue-plate special, would ya?"

Chapter Twenty-Six:

Say lah

vee!

THE REST OF THE DAY was spent in fun up to our ears. We all ate our fill and swilled fifty-fives[1] and played games like red light/green light and washers.[2] Grandpa Homer and Grandpa Virgil supplied the live music, and Mom and Pops danced a slow dance until Pops said Mom kept stepping on his toes.[3] We all gathered around the hippomobile for a sing-along to "Let Me Call You Sweetheart," and Mom told Pops to go easy on the rest of us and to just mouth the words. Then everyone wanted Grandpa Homer and Grandpa Virgil to compose a special hippomobile ballad. They got right on it, but it was us who came up with the opening lines:

Way back when, down Wymore way
Lived a man named Gottfried Schuh

But that's as far as we got because Grandma Mabel came

---

1 Those are root beers.
2 Mom's the Deadeye Dick of Wymore, and everybody always wants to be on her team.
3 Mom said that wasn't true.

by and distracted us with a scrumptious-looking black bottom.[4]

Later that afternoon, when some of us were playing charades and Grandma Ida was trying without much luck to be a teapot, Grandpa Milton bellowed out, "It's over now, Henrietta!" All our heads turned quick. Sure enough, he'd just won his first game of checkers.

Grandma Henrietta said, "I wanna rematch!"

But Grandpa Milton just said, "Read this first." He pulled *How to Win at Checkers* out of his pocket and handed it to her.

And as if that wasn't enough to keep us remembering that day for years to come, something else happened. We lost our sun grins, and even our shadows disappeared from the ground. Grandpa Bert pointed up at the sky and shouted, "Hey, look at that!"

We all looked up, and there it was, a little cloud pretty as a pillow. We all gathered under it best we could, and it dropped down a drizzle on us for a good five minutes. And we were happier than ducks on a pond.

It was the most dramatically sensational and rarely

. . . .

4   That's chocolate ice cream with chocolate syrup.

exquisite day of our lives. Once we were back in our hotel room, it turned out it wasn't even over yet. Mom suggested we pitch the tent and sleep out up on the roof. We just couldn't hardly believe it none. Even when Pops claimed he couldn't pitch a tent on account of his back, Mom just said, "Smitty, get!"

Mom stayed down with us and put us through the wringer. She washed our hair clean to the roots and did a twice-over on our ears until they squeaked like mice. Then she trimmed our claws and was making sure we were brushing our teeth right when Pops yelled that he needed some help. She said she should probably give him a hand, and we didn't exactly hold her back none.

We put on our jammies and made sure they were right-side out for a change. But before we went up to join Mom and Pops, we kneeled down by our window and stuck our noses against the screen and breathed in deep. We were about to say something profound and meaningful, maybe something about dogged determination, but we heard Pops from up on the roof. "Hey, where you turkeys at?" he shouted.

And then we heard Mom. "Yeah, you comin' or ain't ya?"

Mom said "ain't"? Yes, indeed, it was truly a day for the history books.

"We're comin'!" we yelled. We jumped up and ran out of the room and were up on the roof while that four-letter word was still ringing in our ears.

There was still a sliver of sun out, and Pops had the tent set up just right so that when we all sat out in front of it, we were able to look clear out over Wymore and watch the sun go down. By then the town was quiet as a whisper, and the only thing you could hear were the cicadas and a grandpa or two snoring louder than a carpenter saws wood.

Mom sighed and said, "It's gorgeous up here."

And Pops just looked at us and winked.

Then we sat there without saying nothing, just swatting mosquitoes and counting golf carts until the sun dipped all the way down behind Mabel's. Then a funny thing happened. That one last lamppost on the square that'd been flickering suddenly gave off a big buzz and flashed once and then went out. And it was like Wymore disappeared right before our very eyes.

And we said, "Aww!"

And Mom said, "That's too bad."

But Pops just said, "Say lah vee."[5]

And so a second or two later, we did say it: "Lah vee!"

And then we all crawled into our tent and went to sleep.

The End[6]

- -

5 Yet another one of Pops's French phrases. And this one means "That's life."
6 That's what we thought, at least. Read on.

Chapter Twenty-Seven:

Home
of the
Hippo-
mobile

WELL, BOOKS MIGHT END, but life don't. Not even life in Wymore.

We thought you might wanna know what all has happened since then. We've been back in school for a couple months now, and a whole bunch has happened since the end of summer when we finished our story. It started out with that picture of us on the front page of the *McFall Dispatch*. Soon as that paper landed on the porches in McFall, the city folk from up there began traveling down here to have a look at the hippomobile for themselves. And so it was mighty good that Pops had been able to rebuild it back together in a matter of days.[1]

By the time he was done, his back was more thrown out than the dishwater, and he was forced to sleep down in the hotel lobby in our tent for a week, since he couldn't climb any stairs. But the bright side was that the McFallians kept right on coming, and some even stayed for lunch and dessert just like we'd hoped they would. Mom was back from

1   He put in a brake and dusted out the horn so it worked, too.

her summer job by then, and she started helping Grandma Mabel out in the kitchen.

People in McFall must've told folks in Muck City about what they'd seen here in Wymore, and soon enough them Muckers were also paying us a visit. And from there things snowballed in a way ain't no one ever could've expected. Because from Muck City word passed on to the town of Nuckles, and soon we had more Nucklites in town than we knew what to do with. Then came the communities of Slapout and Goobertown. And from there news of the hippomobile somehow crossed the waters of Mud Creek, and before we knew it, the citizens of Yeehaw Junction and Gnaw Bone and Weedpatch were piling into their pickups and taking a trip to Wymore. Then came the Pine Stumpers from Pine Stump, and our town square ain't never been so gritty as it was with all them folks kicking up dust.

By that time Mom was working full-time at Mabel's, and Pops was needed more and more in town to fix things up and keep everything running smooth for the grow-ing number of visitors. And that was even before them two rich-looking reporters in fancy suits came to town to write an article they wanted to call "Thirty-Six Hours in Wymore." And even though it ended up being called "Six Hours in Wymore," the article appeared in a big news-paper, and that sealed it. Pops gave up his trucking job, but not his beret, and he became Wymore's around-the-clock maintenance man. He wore one of them big belts with all the tools stuck in it and not only fixed the screen door at Mabel's and put new bulbs in the streetlamps, but he also strung up Wymore's first traffic light. Because it's like they say, every silver lining has its cloud.

Mom and Pops weren't the only ones with new jobs. One day Grandpa Bert pulled a rack of his leftover clothes out onto the sidewalk and declared himself back in busi-ness. He renamed his store the Hippodashery, and within a week he sold his first shirt. Grandma Francine began offer-ing "Hippo hairdos" at her beauty parlor. Grandma Pearl acquired two more Pioneers and started giving prospecting expeditions in and around Wymore. Anything you found you got to keep, and her business boomed, even though most people just went away with a pocket full of rusty nails. Grandma Mabel tried to come up with a new dish called hippomobile hash, but she was never completely satisfied with the results, and so it never made it onto the menu. Apparently some things just ain't meant to be. Whereas on the other hand, some things are apparently meant to be for a second time. Because now there's even been some talk about refixing back up some of the houses off the square for us to move back into. That way visitors from far off can stay at the Slantey just like in the olden days and carve their names in the wood right alongside Cager, Hepsie, and Zubia.

Well, that leaves the two of us. The first thing we did was organize a field trip to Wymore our third day back in school. We promised our teacher there was a lot of local history to be learned there, and we promised our classmates it'd be even better than an elevator. No one believed us at first, but we made believers outta the whole fifth-grade class, including our teacher, once our bus pulled into town and we gave them a ride around Wymore on the hippomobile.[2] Pops had to do the actual driving, but we were responsible for telling them the whole story about the young man by the name of Gottfried Schuh who one day arrived in Wymore fresh off the boat from a place called Germany. They ate it up, too.

Soon we got so good at flavoring that story that we

. . . .

2 Everyone had to wear a helmet.

were becoming true linguisters just like Grandpa Homer and Grandpa Virgil. And it wasn't long before we began giving tours every Saturday and Sunday afternoon. While Pops drove around the square, and out to the old shoe factory if he thought the hippomobile was up to it that day, we told the visitors the Gottfried Schuh story, and somehow it came out a little different every time. The tour always ended right in front of Mabel's, and to get the visitors in the door, Mom had the idea of offering them a complimentary cup of joe. Nine times out of ten it worked, and another nine times out of ten the customers ordered something else to go with it. Grandma Ida said she hadn't served so many plates of butcher's revenge[3] in years. And one lady, sitting in front of a houseboat,[4] said the dessert was so good that she was gonna bring her knitting club out the following week. And she did, too.

Then one Saturday afternoon as we were getting everybody on board, you won't believe who we saw climb up. It was Fitz, the train engineer! "I was just passin' through

. . . .

3 Meatloaf.
4 That's a banana split.

town," he said. He dug his hand into a bag he had with him and pulled out two hats. They each had MILES wrote on it and fit us perfect. We had him sit up front, and when we got at the corner of Hill Street, we let him blow the horn.

"F-sharp," we said.

Fitz said, "You kids are all right."

We just tipped our hats.

Them hats gave us an idea, too. We called our grandmas together, and they had hats and shirts made up that said I ♥ HIPPOMOBILE on them. Grandpa Bert put them in the window of his Hippodashery, and they sold like hotcakes. Then we contacted Mr. Buzzard, and he delivered us a giant tub of shoe wax and a carton of shoeshine brushes. Because remember all them Gottfrieds down at the old shoe factory? Well, we shined them until our shoulders were as sore as a bump on your head. A few of them Everlasting Shoes went on display at Mabel's, but the rest went on sale, and we sold more Gottfrieds than Gottfried himself ever did.

And that just about puts the lid on this pot of beans. Unless of course you wanna know how we did on our history test. Well, you'd never believe the fun you can have with presidents like John Tyler[5] and James Buchanan[6] once you wrap them up into a good story. In fact, it ain't even gotta be all that good, it's just gotta be a story. Grandpa Chester was right. But in the end, we didn't get an A on our test. We got an A+. And that's because we'd memorized all the middle names, too.

· ·

5   We put a dishrag in his hands and had him wipe down the tables.
6   He was in charge of the place mats.

The End